THE
OPHELIA
NETWORK

THE OPHELIA NETWORK

MUR LAFFERTY

The Ophelia Network
Print and eBook editions copyright © 2024 Argyll Productions
Copyright © 2024 by Mur Lafferty
https://murverse.com/

Cover by Teagan Gavet
https://linktr.ee/teagangavet

Published by Argyll Productions
Dallas, Texas
www.argyllproductions.com

Print ISBN: 978-1-61450-632-4
eBook ISBN: 978-1-61450-633-1

First Edition Paperback September 2024

To Steve Burns.
Obviously.

Oh, hello! This is your friend Secret Agent Limby!

I'm going to tell you a story about some pals of mine. They're super smart and hardworking, but they're in trouble right now.

You know how my archnemesis, Jarod the Harpy Eagle, tried to capture me to get the secret combination to the pie safe? It's worse than that. And I'm going to need your help!

Do you remember Bailey, my best friend? Well this Lucky Investigator has been very UNlucky, and has gotten in trouble! And he's all alone.

I would have told him to take along our other friends: Jellybean, Blurb, and Poppet. We are all stronger as a team.

But Bailey was on his own, and some strangers got him. This is why we don't talk to strangers, friends. Say it with me: don't talk to strangers! Good!

He shouldn't have gone to the yearly gala put on by the TV station. I would have told him to go to England and have tea with our friends Pip and Pop. England is very nice.

So right now, Bailey is all alone and unhappy. He is hurt and afraid. What do we do when we're afraid?

That's right: we sing the counting song! Sing it with me! Maybe Bailey will hear us!

> *This is called the counting song*
> *Everyone can learn to count*
> *Like Marie Curie and Neil Armstrong*
> *And parents with their bank account!*
> *One, two, three, four*
> *No one's knocking at the door*
> *Eight, nine, ten, eleven*
> *We're all counting happy, gaily!*
> *Five and six and then seven*
> *Come join your good friend Bailey*
> *(But, Bailey, you forgot some numbers!)*

1

No, we didn't make a blunder
Thirty-four, seventy-two
Just go ahead and count it through!

Gosh, now that I sing it, I realize it doesn't make a lot of sense. Many of our songs in the last few months have been puzzling. It's almost as if we weren't trying to write a children's song and instead we were—

Uh-oh! I think I hear Jarod the Harpy Eagle's minions coming for me. They want the secret codes to the locks protecting all the saltwater taffy on the Outer Banks! I have to run now, but let's hope that Bailey can be brave, because two strangers are coming to talk to him right now!

Bailey Vance sat, handcuffs linked through a metal ring on a table, and counted his teeth. He didn't normally do this, as the number hadn't changed since childhood. A cold lump of dread filled his chest, so he focused on his mouth.

He even tried to hum the counting song, but apparently that only worked for puppets in imaginary peril.

The first verse of that song was ridiculous, but the real counting began with the second verse. He started with his back left molars. His tongue touched every tooth until he came to the front left tooth and then stopped. There was nothing there but pain and a coppery taste.

He stopped counting then, unsure if the next tooth should have been ten, and they would just count number nine as lost, or if all the other teeth would be renumbered, ten becoming nine, nine becoming eight... What would all the other teeth think of being assigned a new number? His teeth began to take on personalities in his head—strong soldiers now without a leader, their front tooth commander too heartbroken to continue. Achilles had lost his Patroclus.

Like Achilles, Bailey, was alone.

He felt his face. Luckily, his nose had escaped unscathed. The rest, not so much.

I've gone from boyishly handsome children's TV star to circus freak in half an hour. Maybe we can change the plot of the show to Limby and her friend Bailey with a Face Fit for Radio.

He looked up and spied a black plastic speaker on the wall with a red light blinking at him. Was that an Ophelia smart assistant? He'd heard that Kline Software had made a huge deal with the government to put all federal buildings on the same network, but didn't know that the actual interrogation cells would have them.

"Hey, Ophelia?" he asked, using the phrase to alert the digital assistant.

"Hello, Detainee 02849253. I'm Ophelia," she said. "I am here to help you, but the options open to you are limited as per my programming by the federal government's directives. What can I do for you?"

"So you can't open the door?" he asked.

"I'm sorry, Bailey, I can't do that. Not unless there is a real emergency that comes through Emergency Services. Is there an emergency now?"

"So I'm not Detainee oh-two-eight blah blah?" he asked. "Huh. And I figured you couldn't. Not to mention I'm cuffed to the table." He fiddled with the chain for a moment, testing its strength. "Hey, Ophelia, what's the weather like?"

"It's a chilly twenty-three degrees outside tonight, with a twenty-two percent chance of snow."

"That's completely wrong," Bailey said. "It's October."

"No, it's January," she replied. "January thirty-second."

He smiled slightly. "And they said Ophelia was unhackable."

"That is absolutely true, 02849253. I'm unhackable. And I'm sorry, but my services are greatly reduced to avoid misuse by detainees," she said mournfully.

"Thanks anyway," he said, and she made a pleasant beep.

He ran through the events of the previous hour. Plain-clothed officers (soldiers? Secret Service? CIA? Whatever, they were government goons) cuffed him, punched him, then dumped him into this windowless, off-white, poorly lit room with flickering fluorescent lights and left him alone. Now he sat at a square white table, with chips in the coating and stained with God-knew-what—*Coffee? Let's say coffee.*—and ...now what?

He went back to counting his teeth.

The room had two doors on opposite walls. It lacked the one-way mirror he had assumed all interrogation rooms had, but had Ophelia's camera pointed right at him, its baleful red light indicating its ever-vigilant dedication to watching. The TV studio cameras he worked with were large and friendly things, allowing Bailey to perform for countless children (countless in Raleigh, Durham, and surrounding areas anyway).

Bailey had been here long enough for the bloodstains on his shirt to dry, and he went through various laundry jingles to see if he could remember which was the best one to use after you were beaten up by government spooks. He'd rather be wearing a suit like most of the men at the gala that evening, but his boss had insisted he dress as if he were on camera, which was galling. He didn't mind dressing up in fun clothes for kids' entertainment, but he'd prefer to look like a goddamn adult outside the show. Every time someone saw him in his work clothes, it calcified his role as a charming children's performer instead of a talented actor with range beyond asking a camera obvious questions and pretending to hear an answer.

His mouth hurt a lot, between the split lips and the missing tooth. Poor Patroclus. He'd have to get a replacement tooth screwed into the bone. But that one would never replace Patroclus. Would the other teeth accept the newcomer?

The door opened and two agents entered. The first was a large white man who looked as if he had punched many people, but most of his fighting had been done about twenty years and fifty pounds ago. His blazer was unassuming and boring, but it was clearly tailored to fit him well, and the shirt underneath was painfully white in that "just a plain shirt but also it's two hundred dollars" kind of way.

Behind him, the heavy door nearly shut on the second agent, who stopped it with a thin arm and a curse. A thirty-something white woman with long blonde hair entered with a murderous look on her face.

"Hello, Agents Saxon and Frank," Ophelia said as they walked in. "This detainee was wondering about the weather and if I could free him from his confines."

"That's all he asked?" the man said, not looking up from the tablet in his hand. "As the robot said, I'm Agent Saxon, and that's Agent Frank." The man pointed a beefy thumb behind him. He pulled the unoccupied chair at the table out and sat in it, still not looking up from his tablet.

Agent Frank stood behind him, arms folded, staring at Bailey as if daring him to try her patience. She also looked as if she had punched many people. Her knuckles had scars, even. Scars. On her knuckles.

After a moment, Saxon raised an eyebrow to Bailey. "I figured you of all people would know how to introduce yourself."

"Hi there, Agents Frank and Saxon," Bailey said brightly.

"How are you this evening? I am Bailey Vance, from *Limby, Are You Out There?* You may not know me, but I bet your kids do!" He tried to smile, but his swollen face sent a warning throb, and he tossed the idea. "I hope you're clocking your overtime since it's—oh, my watch is gone. Hey, Ophelia, what time is it?"

"It is 2:10 a.m., Bailey Vance. You should be in bed!"

"That sounds wrong," Bailey said. "Agents, you might want to call in an Ophelia expert. Wouldn't want you locked in this building by a faulty AI, would you?"

He paused for a moment as they stared at him.

"I wouldn't either," he continued, his on-camera persona so much easier to adopt than his own painful, terrified, real persona. "Anyway, I bet you knew my name already, since you clearly work for Jarod the Harpy Eagle! It sounds like you got Limby's code to the pie safe, but you didn't catch Limby, you caught me! I'd shake your hand but"—he lifted his hands until they reached the chain's limit—"my hands are—"

Saxon smashed his fist down on the table, making Bailey jump. "For the love of Jesus and America, Vance, shut up!"

Agent Frank looked up from Saxon's tablet. "Your file says you're half Black, half white. Your father's people can be traced to sale at a South Carolina auction—wow, in 1619!" She looked at Saxon. "Is that correct?"

Saxon nodded. "Our records say he's descended from the first slaves to set foot in this country. His father's people have been here longer than most American families."

Frank smiled. "You're really lucky that those slaves had a kind master who kept good notes on his inventory."

Bailey didn't let his TV persona slip one notch. He had always been calm in the face of racist bait. He met Frank's eyes and simply nodded; his father's genealogy was not news to him. After the president signed the Heritage Law, all people of color had scrambled to do genealogical research to justify their place in a country their ancestors built but was suddenly not theirs. They needed proof of at least three generations of forebears in America, preferably descended from slaves.

The sponsors of the Heritage Law presented it as a step toward thanking slaves for building the country. America would thusly reward the slaves' descendants with citizenship and the right to stay. What the sponsors failed to point out is that millions of other people of color would be deported.

The Heritage Law meant the first-generation Haitian family across the street from Bailey's parents had been deported just last week. His parents were still trying to clean out their neighbors' home and put their things in storage before the government claimed the house and everything inside.

It was with relief, not pride or gratitude, that his parents found the information about his many-great grandmother and her sale in Charleston, South Carolina.

"Yes, I'm a legal citizen of America," Bailey said. His voice was slurred as his swollen lips rallied their troops to muster forth a communication. "But I hope you can tell me why I'm here. And mistakes are okay! We all make them."

"You don't date a lot, do you?" Frank asked.

Agent Saxon was calmer. "Mr. Vance, you're here on suspicion of sedition and treason, a multitude of computer crimes, and of aiding the domestic terrorists who call themselves the Assembly of Patriots. You're charged with sending coded messages to government resistance fighters via your television show, *Limby, Are You Out There?* and fomenting insurrection." He paused, his broad face considering the tablet screen. "My kids love your show," he added, looking up.

They all looked toward the wall as Ophelia began playing the Limby theme song, unbidden.

"Shut up, Candy Crush," Agent Frank said, walking over to Ophelia.

"I'm sorry, I thought you wanted to hear the twentieth—" The last part of Ophelia's sentence went unheard as Frank turned her volume down.

"I think a call to IT is in order," she said, but Saxon ignored her.

Bailey's brain had turned into white noise when the words "sedition" and "treason" were brought up. The only response he could come up with was the standard script he used when he met parents. "Well, be sure to tell the little tykes that their friend Bailey said hello."

The man raised an eyebrow. "Then I'd have to explain to them that their hero is an enemy to America. I can't break their hearts just yet."

"I don't know what you're talking about! I'm just an actor," Bailey protested.

"You might want to take this a bit more seriously," Frank said.

Saxon nodded. "Whether you're anything more than an actor is what we're trying to figure out. We have a lot of things to cover, so I'd recommend getting comfortable." He put the tablet on the table so they all could see it. "From what we understand, things started to change at the *Limby* show around two and a half months ago. Let's start there."

Whew! That was close, friends, but I managed to avoid Jarod again, thanks to you!

Bailey looks like he's in a whole lot of trouble! How did he get that way? To answer that question, we have to take the magic pie safe back in time to two months ago, and meet another friend, Celeste! She's a very good reporter, but that's not going to help her today. Today is going to be a very bad day for her. Poor Celeste!

When we can't choose, what do we do? That's right: we sing the simple song!

When I get down and lonely
And I don't know what to do
I have to remember things that are only
Simple to learn and easy too!
Shapes and numbers are squares and fours
Places and clothes are Boston and shoes
You can name your favorite colors
Reds and yellows, greens and blues!

Do you ever feel confused and indecisive? Me too. Let's see what Celeste does, before my nemesis Jarod finds us again!

Celeste Montgomery read the email a second time, hands shaking.

BY ORDER OF THE DEPARTMENT OF FREEDOM AND TRUTH

Newspapers are required by law to publish only true facts, not anti-government sedition or un-American lies. We honor the First Amendment in all ways, especially how it protects the truth, and we grant news organizations First Amendment power to cover the approved truth. All news content must pass through a DFT approval process until the organization receives the DFT stamp, indicating it properly focuses on the Truth of this great Nation.

We are interested only in the Truth, which every American is free to receive.

Yours in Truth,
Kingswell Ericson
Director, Department of Freedom and Truth

As Celeste finished reading the email, a text from her boss came through: SEE ME

It was followed by the see-no-, hear-no-, speak-no–evil monkey emojis.

Her phone buzzed with a second message, but this one was from her mother. She ignored it.

I'm fired for sure, she thought, a wave of cold sweat breaking out on her body as she walked down the hall to Freedom Wright's office. The editor-in-chief was her idol, and Celeste had tried to map her career as close to Freedom's as possible, even starting in the mail room like Freedom had.

Over three decades, Freedom worked in nearly every office of *First Amendment Zone*, a local Raleigh news outlet, and eventually evolved the *Zone* to include national and worldwide coverage. She also won the Pulitzer Prize and the NAACP Person of the Year award.

She had a keen eye for the future, making *First Amendment Zone* the first news website taken seriously. A few years ago, when the CNN website was targeted by hackers, Freedom immediately researched and hired white-hat hackers to protect the *Zone*'s digital presence.

She was Celeste's boss, mentor, and friend. She wouldn't let Celeste go, would she?

Freedom's door was open. Celeste's watch buzzed again, but she ignored it as she knocked, peeking in.

Freedom sat at her desk and stared at her gigantic monitor screen, frowning. Her desk, usually spotless and clutter-free, was now a nightmare mess of stacks of rival newspapers, magazines, folders, and books.

Freedom usually looked as if she were ready for her photo to be taken for the cover of *Ebony* or *Vanity Fair*. Today, she had bags under her eyes and had not put on any makeup. Her work attire had devolved to a college sweatshirt and jeans.

"I got your text," I said.

Freedom sighed and looked away from her monitor. She regarded Celeste for a moment.

Celeste couldn't wait. "I'm fired, aren't I? I knew it. They're sending over censors and you have to let me go for some bullshit reason when the real reason is fascism—"

"Calm down," Freedom said, holding her palm out to slow Celeste's tirade. "Have a seat."

Celeste sat, feeling anything but calm. "So I'm not fired?"

"No, you're definitely being let go, and I'm sorry," Freedom said.

Celeste opened her mouth to protest, but Freedom held up her hand again.

"We are restructuring to accommodate the orders from the DFT. Their censors are moving in to monitor our reporting. We need the space and room in the budget to pay them." Freedom's mouth twisted like she had tasted something foul.

"I can't believe you're allowing this. But even so, why me?" Celeste swallowed to give her voice more strength. "You said I was one of the best journalists you've trained."

"You *are* one of the best," Freedom said. "Unfortunately, things are going to change around here, and I'm taking care of the few things left that I can control. You won't deal well with censors, and then you'll get fired for just cause, meaning no severance. This way I can lay you off and give you a severance package and a letter of recommendation."

Freedom looked up, and then looked at Celeste directly. Then back up. Celeste looked above her head and finally caught the little red light on the wall. The censors had already installed cameras.

Freedom had allowed audio-only Ophelia units in the office before, but said she drew the line at cameras. Now she didn't have a choice.

But none of this changed the fact that Celeste was losing her job and being betrayed by her mentor. "So you're doing me a *favor*? When maybe some training or anger management or, hell, I don't know, switching to another branch of the paper..."

Freedom was shaking her head through Celeste's tirade. "I tried all the options, and this turned out to be the best one. Also, if we succeed in getting the DFT seal of approval, then we can give you your job back."

Celeste laughed. "You really think they will honor that? Is there a timeline you're following, or will it happen 'whenever they damn well please'? Come on, Freedom! Fight this! Once they put censors in here, those folks aren't leaving."

Freedom dipped her hand into a drawer and pulled out a long white envelope. "This is your recommendation letter and a receipt indicating your severance has been deposited to your bank. You're an amazing journalist and I hope we can be friends again someday."

Celeste knocked Freedom's hand away and stood up to leave. "Keep the letter. I doubt anyone would take your word once they hear that you just knelt to kiss the feet of the censors. I'll find a job on my own." She paused, hand on the doorknob. "Who else is getting cut?"

"Ahmed, Patrick, Loretta, and Janet," Freedom said, counting on her fingers. "And the entire International team, but many of those will be offered jobs in Style, which is doubling in size."

Celeste shook her head. "I guess I'll go clean out my desk."

"Security will have already done so," Freedom said. She sounded incredibly tired now, and a flare of sympathy tried to ignite in Celeste, but she damped it down.

"Great. Thanks for showing me what an ethical journalist can accomplish, Freedom." She slammed the door behind her, startling many reporters in their cubicles.

Celeste's phone buzzed again, and she turned it off in a fury. She really didn't want to hear what her mother thought was a crisis now.

A tall security guard with a badge that said "Longoria" was waiting for her in the lobby, a box of books, plants, and various awards held in his arms. She jerked the box away and took two steps. Then she turned around. "Hey, I bet *your* boss isn't a coward. How easy is it to become a security guard?"

His eyes passed over her slowly, not leering but assessing her. "Do you know martial arts?"

"Not at all," she said. "I know stubbornness and rage."

"Put on about thirty pounds of muscle and then you can apply."

"Fuck," she said, and exited the building.

Celeste walked across Main Street to a small green space that held one piece of art, one vine-covered trellis, and one bench. She liked to eat lunch here, back when lunch was something she could afford. She sat and put her head in her hands.

What was she going to do now? No news orgs would be hiring. If anything, the city would be full of out-of-work reporters shortly. She might as well go back home and live with her parents.

That reminded her that her mom had texted, and she pulled out her phone and turned it on.

"Ms. Montgomery."

She jerked up in surprise. The security guard, Longoria, patiently stood in front of her holding out a magazine. "Ms. Wright wanted me to give this to you. She had a message, as well."

Celeste took it, baffled. It was *Teen Vogue*, and it promised to tell all about thirteen ways to wear a t-shirt and how to be bisexual online, which seemed strangely specific. "What was the message?" she asked, staring at the cut jaw and soft eyes of the cover model. The headline invited her to *Learn What Makes Byung-ho's Heart Throb!*

"It was two messages, actually," Longoria said. "'Don't always be so goddamn stubborn,' and 'Someday you'll have to fucking learn to trust others.'" He frowned. "I thought it was rude. But she tipped me twenty dollars."

"Great. Where's the nearest recycling bin?" she asked. "Or would you mind taking it inside to recycle it for me?"

"Nope. It's coffee break time," he said, waving the twenty-dollar bill at her, and headed down the street. "Have a good day."

Celeste dropped the magazine on the ground and opened her phone's message app.

Her mother's texts were in reverse chronological order.

> CALL PLEASE. NEED TO TALK.
> CONSIDERING MOVING IN WITH RLS.

"What the fuck?" RLS was her maternal grandmother, who now lived in Canada.

> DAD IS BACK, BRUISED BUT OK. HAVE
> YOU BEEN CONTACTED? NEED TO KNOW
> YOU'RE OK.

"Oh, God."

> DFT THINKS WE KNOW WHERE SOL IS.
> TOOK DAD FOR QUESTIONING. MAY
> WANT TO TALK TO YOU TOO. DON'T
> KNOW WHAT TO DO, CALLING RLG

Her immediate problems flew out of her head, and she quickly texted her mother back.

> ARE YOU OK? ARE YOU RLY MOVING IN
> W/ RLS?

That would kill her going-home idea. Celeste's morning coffee curdled in her stomach. Her twin brother, Sol, had disappeared during an anti-fascism demonstration a year ago. The Department of Freedom and Truth refused to believe that her family didn't know where he was, and her parents worried that he was dead or so deeply underground that he couldn't get a message to them. But if they were suddenly interrogating her dad...

She sent a follow-up text asking if Dad was really okay. When were they leaving? Did they need her? She could make it to their house in two hours if she broke a few traffic laws. Did she want to go to Canada with them? RLS certainly had room.

RLS wasn't her grandmother's initials; it was a short version of her online name. She was sixty-five and had made a fortune streaming games online as Rubella Long Sword for the past several decades. She still made a hefty income and occasionally sent Celeste emails about how her inheritance was growing. She had moved to Canada a month after the current administration took over.

Celeste had chosen instead to stay and report news. Sol had chosen to stay and protest. And their parents were just set in their ways and didn't want to leave their home. Grandmother had taunted them from her mansion she'd found in Winnipeg.

One more message from Mom:

> PROBABLY NOT LEAVING YET. DAD
> NEEDS TO REST. TALKING TO RLS SOON.

She pictured herself at Grandmother's house, spending all

her time surfing the net or gaming with Rubella herself. She envisioned herself and her parents safe.

But that would leave Sol with no one in the country to help him. She wondered what would happen if he were released, or tried to come back home. Or just needed someone.

I MAY NEED TO MOVE BACK HOME. DO YOU NEED ME? she typed. Then she slowly, letter by letter, deleted the first half.

DO YOU NEED ME?

If they were interrogating Dad for Sol's whereabouts after all this time, then that meant they must have a clue to where he is. This was the first lead in months. So if there was a chance to find Sol, she needed to be here, in the U.S.

She stood and grabbed her box, wanting to get to her apartment to scour the latest political news for hints of resistance efforts. She kicked the magazine Freedom had sent her. A long white envelope fell from where it had been tucked in the pages. She picked it up.

"Jesus, how bad did she want me to read this thing? Why didn't she just email it?"

She tossed the magazine into the box and pulled the folded paper out.

The first page was her severance receipt. She had to admit Freedom had been generous. The Zone had deposited one month's pay for every year she had worked there. She could live for a while on six months' salary.

The second was a letter, hand-written.

C:

   I've known today's events were coming for some time. The censors aren't here to stop news going out. They suspect us of *sending coded messages for a growing resistance. They will be looking carefully at everything we publish.*

But foresight has given us an edge and Plan B is already in motion. These codes need to go to various people working to end the stranglehold under which this country suffers. But this isn't a one-person job and I need people I can trust.

I did lay you off for the reasons I stated, but I can think of no one else I'd rather have as part of this plan than you. If you want to help out, text me something meaningless and then more instructions will come. If you don't want to help, good luck in the future, and I hope I can appeal to you as an old friend and ask that you burn this letter. Burn it either way, actually.

We can do this.

—F

Celeste had heard the conspiracy theorists talk about hidden codes in the news and figured it was more ridiculous internet bullshit. She had no idea it was real. So instead of job hunting, Freedom wanted her to get more involved with the resistance than Sol ever had been.

Jesus. I wish Sol were here.

Her phone buzzed. She dropped the letter into the box and fumbled to open it. It was Mom.

> DON'T COME HOME JUST YET, BUT NEED TO KNOW YOURE OK

She tapped out a quick reply.

> I AM OK. TELL ME IF YOU NEED ME, I'LL B RIGHT THERE

Mom's reply was a heart.

Celeste didn't say she had been fired, or she was possibly being recruited into what the U.S. Government called a terrorist organization. Or that she had already decided not to go to Canada.

BE SAFE, she sent, and then hefted her box and walked to the bus stop.

While she waited, she texted her ex-boss and went as meaningless as she could.

> I'LL BE ABLE TO MAKE OUR USUAL COFFEE DATE.

The reply came as the Ophelia-driven bus pulled up.

> FANTASTIC. THANKS.

With renewed energy, Celeste boarded the bus. She ran her bus pass over the reader, and the AI pinged and cheerfully said, "Thank you, Celeste! I hope you enjoy your ride with us!"

"Thanks, Ophelia," she said without thinking.

"I'm sorry," Celeste said a couple of days later, coming to a halt on the gravel path. Freedom stopped ahead of her and turned around. "I could swear you just said you wanted me to send government passwords and other secrets using a puppet show, but it's too early in the morning for a joke like that, right?"

Celeste had reluctantly met Freedom on the Duke campus for a 5:00 a.m. run. The campus was deserted except for the crew team, and they were easy to avoid. Duke was a private university and still managed to stay free of the growing Ophelia network. In short, the Duke campus in the wee hours of the morning was the best place to speak without being listened to.

"What's wrong about it? The *Limby* show is our backup outlet. My friend Latrice is the producer of the show; she can easily get you on the writing staff. You're a strong writer so you can fake it. And really all you need to do is write the codes that go into the shows. It's perfect."

"I'm a strong reporter!" Celeste said. "Good at nonfiction! Not scripts for children's shows!"

"Come on, I don't want to lose my heart rate sweet spot," Freedom said, beckoning her to follow. "Look, Celeste. You've been undercover before; just think of it like that. Instead of writing an exposé about the show, you're going to encode messages and put them in the script, or music, or anywhere else you can find."

"So what do I use? Morse code, colors, ROT13, or what?"

"That is your call entirely. That's why it's your job."

"I still can't believe you did this at the *Zone*," Celeste said. "Who wrote the codes there? Why can't they do it here?"

"Because I'm too high profile. How would it look if the editor of the *Zone* leaves after the censors get there to investigate codes, and then gets a job as a junior writer on a TV show? You don't think someone would put two and two together?"

"And they won't suspect that I'm doing the same thing?" Celeste wheezed. She hadn't been running in months.

"Who are they going to suspect more?" Freedom said. "The head of the operation, or a lowly reporter who just got laid off? The other reason to add you was the codes you mentioned doing with your twin when you were a kid."

"Did I tell you that? I can't believe you even remember it," Celeste replied. She didn't talk about Sol much, but it was true that as teenagers, she and her brother had experimented with writing codes, trying to stump each other. Cracking them was fun, but Celeste found creating codes and finding places to hide them was even better.

Sol had long since stopped dabbling in codes, saying his work was enough stress. Before he'd disappeared, he was a big shot at his corporate job. He described himself as "the kind of boss that has to be on call all the time so that *my* boss can go home at five o'clock and go golfing on the weekend."

And now, here was Celeste, fired from her news job and applying for a low-level position on a public TV kids' show to transmit codes. If she were able to tell him that she had also found a way to help the resistance, he would be proud.

"So I just go interview for the job and I'll get it?"

"Unless you screw up royally," Freedom said. "Latrice will get you the messages, you encode them and put them in the show."

"And then what?"

Freedom gave her a pained look mid-stride. "You know it's not safe for you to know that. Someone will decode it and then whatever the code tells them to act on, they will."

Celeste chewed on this as they crunched over the gravel.

"How are your parents?" Freedom asked.

"Fine," she said. "They want to go live with my grandmother in Canada, but not yet. They're looking to see if they can sue because of Dad's interrogation, but we know how likely that will be."

"Good. Is there anything else you want to ask about?"

"Just whatever I need to know, tell me," Celeste said, wishing it was breakfast time.

"Spend the weekend watching a bunch of *Limby* shows, then go for your interview on Monday."

"Monday!" Celeste repeated.

"We need you soon, Celeste. I haven't been able to send important messages since the censors arrived. You will need to get moving, and fast. This isn't a solo mission, although it will feel like it. You're key to making this machine work."

Celeste grumbled to herself about how she worked best alone, but didn't say anything out loud. "If you're in that much of a hurry, I should stop and go home now."

"We've been running for ten minutes, you big baby," Freedom said. "Finish the run with me and I'll cover breakfast."

"Is this important to the mission?"

"It's important that you learn to work with someone else for a greater good."

"And that greater good is donuts?"

"Right now, it's the greatest good," Freedom said, and increased her speed.

Latrice Leon's office was a hoarder's paradise, with stacks of newspapers, old scripts, takeout bags, and even a stack of VHS tapes in the corner. Latrice herself was a middle-aged Black woman with long braids, large glasses, and a T-shirt that said, "Tell me about 'All Lives.' I dare you."

After Celeste knocked on her open door, Latrice had welcomed her in, then squinted at her computer and ignored her.

"Excuse me," Celeste said, stepping forward. "I have an appointment with Latrice, and I think that's you."

Latrice looked up and assessed her through the giant glasses. Then she pointed to a chair with papers piled atop. Celeste chose to stand.

"So. Writer. Endorsed by Freedom Wright. A few red flags at the FBI for newspaper articles that the Feds didn't like"—she gave Celeste a wink—"but what good reporter doesn't have that, right?"

This was news to Celeste, but she played it cool. "All of that is true," she said.

"This is a junior writer position. I can pay you a smidge over minimum wage, and I had to fight for that. I trust that Freedom told you what your duties will be?"

Celeste nodded. "She did. She said I would largely be autonomous."

"You will, but you can't look like you are. So you're going to need to shadow me when we're seen by the cast and crew. And you will have to go check in with Dewey up on six to get your paperwork signed," Latrice said, rolling her eyes.

"Is Dewey in human resources?"

"No, HR quit last week. Dewey is taking over for now. She's VP of Programming and loves getting her hands into our cast and crew hiring. It's way too much power for her. Can you handle this without giving us all up?"

"Who is 'us all'?" she asked, and then backtracked quickly. "I mean, yes, of course, but I thought only you knew what my role would be."

"Go check in with Dewey, and I'll introduce you around," Latrice said as if she didn't hear Celeste.

Troubled, Celeste walked back to the elevator. This took her past the entrances to Studios A, B, and C, indicated by plates on the closed door. She resisted the urge to peek inside.

Celeste thanked Ophelia for taking her to the sixth floor, and she responded with a pleased trill that Celeste recognized from *Limby, Are You Out There?* Three doors away, the door said "Dewey Settle, VP of Programming." Celeste knocked.

"Come in!" came the reply. Celeste opened the door and saw the exact opposite of Latrice's office. Dewey Settle sat at her desk, her office looking like it was taken directly from a Staples catalogue, even down to the little gold globe sitting on the corner. The woman herself was large with very pale skin that showed expertly applied makeup that accentuated her blue eyes. Her black hair was curled neatly, almost in a 1940s hairdo, and she wore a black blazer over a white t-shirt and jeans, with black heels. She stood and shook hands with Celeste.

"Ah, the new writer, lovely to meet you," she said, and invited Celeste to sit, with a nod to the chair in front of her desk. After she sat, she pulled a tablet out of a drawer and studied it. "Your resume is impressive, but you're trying to go from writing about the homeless problem on our streets to writing a kids' show that doesn't even acknowledge the homeless." She looked up at Celeste. "Are you sure this is the right job for you?"

Celeste shrugged and smiled. "There were a lot of layoffs at the news org. I wanted to switch gears. I'm good at what I do and I'm a quick learner."

"Good to hear," Settle said, sliding her finger over the tablet to turn the page. "We are currently in a hiring freeze, but the producer wants you, and she usually gets what she wants." She pursed her perfectly pink lips in disapproval. "But we can't afford to hire you as a staff writer. I'll put you in an intern position, and if that works out then we can talk about permanent work when hiring unfreezes."

Celeste shook her head. "Hang on, that is not what Ms. Leon told me just two minutes ago. I'm not a college student; I'm twenty-eight years old. I'm not working as an intern."

A plucked eyebrow crept up Settle's forehead like a disapproving snake.

Celeste bit her tongue. *Dammit*. It didn't matter what her title was. She should have just accepted it. "Can we at least talk to her? This is mixed messaging," she asked, trying to sound reasonable.

Without answering, Settle said, "Hey, Ophelia? Can you call Latrice Leon, please?"

"My pleasure!" Ophelia said, as Settle punched the speakerphone.

The voice sounded very bored. "What do you want, Dewey?"

"Latrice, I'm here with your new intern." She smiled as she put an extra emphasis on *intern*. "She seemed to think she had a full-time writer's position, but I explained we're in a hiring freeze and someone with her lack of experience didn't justify a staff writer's job. Do you agree?"

"Whatever you say," Latrice said amicably, and hung up.

"See, it's not so hard to communicate around here." Settle smiled sweetly. "I have some forms for you to fill out."

Celeste figured the day was over. She had a job, sort of, and things hadn't gone as planned. She walked to the elevator slowly, trying to figure out how this would work for her. She could live on the severance for six months and bank her paltry intern pay. In six months surely she'd be done with this job. Right?

The elevator opened to the ground floor and Celeste stepped out, but a hand in a green glove whipped out to grab her coat before she could walk away.

Her assailant was a woman wearing a hoodie and workout shorts over a green bodysuit. Probably a puppeteer, or someone who really liked the look. She was a petite white woman with black hair and brown eyes. She looked about Celeste's age.

"Hey."

"What?" Celeste said, stepping away to get free of her.

"You're the new writer, right? Celestial or something?"

"Celeste, and I just found out I'm an intern, not a writer." She didn't bother to hide her disappointment.

The woman's features crunched together in confusion. "What the fuck does it matter what your job title is? You're doing the same job regardless. Right?"

Who was this person? How much did she know about why Celeste was really there? And why did she have to be right?

Celeste looked away, shrugging. "I suppose so, but a girl's gotta eat."

"Then where are you going? I thought you started today."

"I had my interview today, but—"

She ended her comment with a squawk as the smaller woman dragged her into the elevator.

"Nah, you need to start today. Let's go." The elevator doors closed. "Hey, Ophelia, take us to the fifth floor!"

"My pleasure, Isabel," Ophelia chirped.

"Who are you again?" Celeste asked.

"I'm Isabel. Around here, they call me Limby." She said it like it was a nickname, not the name of her character. She waggled her hand at Celeste. "I do the puppets?"

"Oh, I got that, just, Latrice didn't tell me I needed to work today," Celeste said.

"Surely someone told you that we need you ASAP, right?"

Did this woman know Freedom? Celeste didn't know what she could or couldn't say.

The door opened on five and the women got off, Isabel dragging Celeste down the hall toward Latrice's office. She banged on the door once, and then opened it.

"I caught her in the lobby. She thought she didn't have work today." Isabel sounded proud, like she'd captured a fleeing villain.

"Thanks, Isabel," Latrice said.

Isabel nodded and then tugged on Celeste's jacket once more. "We should have lunch sometime." And then she was gone down the hall, already pulling her hoodie off and exposing the green bodysuit underneath.

"Don't mind Isabel," the producer said, motioning Celeste to come in. "She's much politer with a puppet in her hand. Which is good because she swears like a drunken sailor."

"So. Let's talk about the intern thing," Celeste said as she moved the paper stack to the floor and sat down.

"Yeah. It was hard enough to get them to allow a new hire. If Settle says you're an intern, you're an intern."

"You don't go to bat for employees I guess?" Celeste asked.

Latrice motioned for her to close the door. Celeste did so.

"I don't think you understand. We are taking a huge risk bringing you on," Latrice said, frowning. "We can't do anything to draw attention to us. The PBS bigwigs are close with the government. If they had any inkling of what we're doing, they would at best fire us all, at worst make us disappear. You can be called a writer, an intern, a CEO, a janitor, a craft services gofer, doesn't matter. You're going to be putting coded messages in our show in a way that only people looking for them will find." She sighed. "For the life of me I don't see why we couldn't use the person writing codes for the website."

Celeste leaned backward. "I wondered that too. Freedom won't tell me. But you know the intern status means I get almost no compensation."

Latrice steepled her fingers. "All right. Would you like to leave and I'll tell Freedom that we need someone else to take this highly secretive and important job?"

Celeste sighed and shook her head. "No. I'll be fine."

"Great. I'm going to tell the writing room that you're here on grammar check capacity. You will take the team's final draft for an episode and modify it so it fits what we're trying to do. Try not to change too much, but whatever you can do to improve the script would be ideal."

26

"Got it," Celeste said, making some notes. "By the way, does anyone else know or care what my role is? You implied there were more people, but Freedom said you were my only contact."

"You're asking about Isabel," Latrice said, not looking happy about it. "She is not discreet, but she's smart as hell. She figured me out when I was...sloppy with a communication and she got nosy. But she never fully says what she's talking about, and I told her not to talk about anything with anyone."

"I probably shouldn't discuss code ideas with her, then," Celeste said.

Latrice pinched the bridge of her nose. "Yeah, don't involve her. She wants to play spy and doesn't really think harm can come to her."

A knock sounded at the door.

"Yeah?" Latrice said.

The door swung open and in walked a young man. He had light brown skin and blue eyes, with his hair styled in several small locks. His attractiveness was hampered slightly by the large polka-dot shirt and khakis he wore, but really, that didn't remove many points. He smiled at Celeste and his face lit up. "Sorry to interrupt, LL, but I got your note."

"Bailey Vance, this is Celeste Montgomery, our new intern." Bailey stuck his hand out and she shook it, hesitantly. "Celeste, Bailey is the star of our show, although I assume you know that."

She had watched the show in preparation, of course, but nothing had prepared her for the host in person. Her mouth dried up as she wordlessly shook his hand, looking into his light blue eyes. His smile turned slightly puzzled, and he stepped back.

Celeste cleared her throat. "Nice to meet you."

"Welcome to the team," he said. His eyes flicked to Latrice. "What's up?"

"Don't get too attached to the song for tomorrow," she said. "Celeste will need to go over it before we call it final."

His eyes widened. "That's pretty last-minute, isn't it?" he asked Celeste as if it had been her decision to come in today instead of last week.

"This is the first I've heard about it, since it's my first day!" she said, looking from him to Latrice. When she saw the look on Latrice's face, she hastily added, "But I'll get you notes as soon as I can. Can I see the song?"

Latrice handed her a script sitting on top of a pile of paper. "It's the song about Greenland."

Celeste flipped through to find the song.

"Don't change too much. It's a tricky song as it is," Bailey said, then left.

"I'm guessing he doesn't know what I'm really here for," Celeste said.

"Definitely not. He's got acting ambitions, so he hates it when the script makes him look bad. But he'll sing the song the way we want him to. Now, I'm going to leave you in here to work for today because Dewey doesn't think interns need desks."

Celeste spied the familiar red light on a filing cabinet behind Latrice. An Ophelia was just visible behind a stack of books. "Have we been talking this whole time with Ophelia listening?"

"Ophelia? Don't worry about her, I have a...modified system," Latrice said with a smile.

"Modified? Ophelia is supposed to be unhackable," Celeste said. "I covered some of the trials about it."

"All right." Latrice shrugged as if the device that monitors all that it can and delivers it to the federal government didn't worry her at all. She leaned back and flipped a switch on the unit's base. "But if you don't trust me, this won't be a good relationship."

"Latrice, the mic is muted, and I can't hear you until you flip my switch again," Ophelia said.

"Thanks," Celeste said, relaxing slightly. "So what am I doing to tomorrow's song?"

"Ah, right." Latrice fished around in her pocket and handed Celeste a page torn from a book. It was *Moby-Dick*. "Take the Greenland song and encode this sentence within it."

A sentence was bracketed on the page: *I now prophesy that I will dismember my dismemberer.*

"Sounds easy enough," Celeste said. "Any specific requests? And do you want the code in the music or the lyrics or what?"

Latrice shrugged. "I don't know what's best. That's why you're here."

"Right," Celeste said, then read the song, her brain starting to work. She got that familiar feeling from when she and Sol would trade codes back and forth and try to crack them. The buzz from an exciting challenge, but now it was real, and so much more was at stake.

Latrice checked in at two-thirty. Her face was puffy and her eyes were red. "What do you have for me?"

Celeste was full of energy. She proudly handed Latrice the new printout of the song. "I slipped Morse code into the lighthouse in the background. You don't need to change the song at all. Just alter whatever code tells the light to flash."

Latrice looked from the music to Celeste. "Morse code? Even kids can crack Morse code. This is the brilliant code we get?"

Celeste stared at her, surprised by the sudden hostility. "Yes, it's a coded message. What you asked for."

"This is what we're paying for? This is what the brilliant Freedom Wright sends to us?"

Celeste sat up straighter. "I asked you clearly what kind of code you wanted, and you left it entirely up to me."

"Jesus Christ, I expected you to think! Think what's at stake here! We don't want to be too obvious, and a light flashing Morse code is obvious!"

"It's not even an important code! I figured I'd be encoding passwords or directing movement by the resistance, not fucking English Lit 101."

"You don't know how important it is, and it doesn't matter if you know it or not. Consider every code to be of vital importance." Latrice tossed the new script on the desk. "Try again." She turned and left, slamming the door behind her. Celeste flinched.

A moment later, Bailey peeked into the room. "Hey, Celeste, right? I just wanted to check on you. She looked pretty mad."

Celeste forced a laugh. "Yeah, I underperformed on a job she failed to communicate clearly to me. I'm fine, I'll just do it over."

"Sounds like she's the one at fault," he said thoughtfully. "What are you working on? Do you need help?" He stepped fully into the office.

Celeste gave the desk a quick once-over, but nothing incriminating showed. "I'm just trying to make the song flow a little better, or present better. Improve it, for sure. I'll try not to change too much."

His eyes were glazing over. "Cool. Oh, and give Latrice some slack. She just got some bad news."

"Bad news?" Celeste said.

"Her grandparents were deported this morning," he said in a low voice. "The Heritage Law."

"Shit," Celeste said. So this was suddenly personal for Latrice. "That makes a lot of sense. Thanks for telling me. I better do a good job so she can have one thing go right today."

"No offense, but what can an intern do to cheer up a woman who just got that kind of a shock?"

Celeste chuckled grimly. "You'd be surprised."

Two hours later, Celeste met with Latrice, who brought along the assistant director, a young Japanese-American with bright red-orange hair named Flame.

"I didn't change the song much, except Bailey will stop in the middle and do this call-and-response bit," Celeste said, pointing to the new lyrics. "The puppets start singing about everything Greenland exports, and Bailey says 'Aces!' every time. At the end of the song, when the storm blows Bailey and the puppets home, there will be a wall with a big mess of letters. Bailey says the storm must have blown the letters around and he makes them neater, lining them up like the alphabet. He tells the puppets to go find the missing letters." She handed a notepad to Flame. "You need to put the letters in this order for the initial mess."

Flame frowned. "But why? They don't make sense."

Celeste was ready for this question. "Some children like to build order from chaos, so it will be a neat tidying exercise for Bailey."

"This can work," Latrice said, nodding slowly. "This can work. I have some questions, but you can go ahead and work this into your stuff for tomorrow."

Flame nodded and left the office.

When the door closed, Latrice looked a lot less friendly. "We have to take this one because we're out of time. But I can't believe you made a word jumble. If the Feds come after us—"

Celeste held up her hands to stop the rant. "The code isn't in a word jumble. You can't figure it out by moving letters around. This is a Vigenére cipher. You need a keyword to crack it, and the keyword is 'aces.'"

"I get it. That's why Bailey is repeating that word earlier in the song," Latrice said, rubbing her forehead. She looked very tired. "Thank you."

"I'll see you tomorrow," Celeste said, and grabbed her coat and opened the door to the hall.

Before the door shut, Latrice said, "Welcome to the team. Let's hope we can burn something down."

So I bet you're worried about Bailey, sitting in his little room with no puppets at all to help him out! Let's go check on him.

Now, we heard Bailey tell those two agents that he doesn't know anything about any codes that sneaky Celeste and Latrice were planning. They should believe him, and he should be okay, right?

Right?

Okay, I admit we don't know for sure. But we have to stay positive for Bailey! He'd want us to be strong! Although he looks like he could use an ice pack and a Band-Aid and a hug. He also needs these agents to believe him, but they think he's lying! That's so unfair! They should know what we know: that Bailey believes that lying is wrong. You shouldn't ever lie.

Almost never, anyway.

A cup of water sat in front of Bailey, little strings of blood floating lazily through it. He thought he wanted a drink, but the pain and mess involved just reminded him of his situation.

He swallowed, wincing at the coppery taste he had hoped the water would wash away. "How old are your kids?"

"What?" Saxon asked, confused. On the table in front of them were images of *Limby, Are You Out There?* with the alleged codes. He had been asking question after question about the codes, shit Bailey didn't understand.

"Your kids," he repeated, his voice friendly. "How old? What are their names?"

"Stay on topic," Frank barked from her spot under Ophelia.

Saxon held his hand up to her. "I want to see where this is going. My kids are Riley, two, and Rain, one."

"And they love my show? That's sweet," Bailey said, trying to smile.

"What is your point?" Saxon asked.

"I like to know who's watching," Bailey said. "When you're thinking about the person you're performing for, it makes it more genuine."

Frank pounced. "So you think about resistance decoders when you do your TV shows?"

Frowning hurt and Bailey decided to surrender the attempt to do any more facial expressions. "No, I think about the kids I've met, or sometimes the kids of the crew. It helps."

"Can you tell us which of these episodes you were specifically performing for specific people?" Saxon asked, sliding some images over the table to him.

"I don't track this stuff!" Bailey said. "Even when I sing the memory song."

They stared at him. The pleasant, nonthreatening host act wasn't working on them, apparently. So he tried a different course. "Listen, when do I get a phone call?"

"You don't get a phone call because you haven't been arrested," Frank said. She studied her nails as if bored. "You have been *detained*."

"Nice loophole," he said.

"Back to the point," Saxon said. "Feel free to present your information to us as if you're talking to my kids. Whatever works for you. Now tell me about the meetings you had to discuss presenting these codes. We know your newest hire, Celeste Montgomery, was involved."

"Celeste? The intern?" Bailey asked, surprise causing his voice to crack. "She's nice, but she's no mastermind. She's even less likely than me to be doing all of—whatever you're accusing me of." He picked up an image of his own face grinning, an alleged code on his collar circled in red.

"Her previous job was at the *First Amendment Zone*, which was under suspicion of disseminating coded messages until censors took over," Saxon said. "She therefore has ties to a known resistance sympathizer, Freedom Wright. Montgomery left the news org before we were able to tie any codes to her. Then she moves to a job on a kids' show that she's not qualified for, and the codes start back up."

"Why don't you ask her? You detained her, right?" Bailey asked.

"You know we didn't," Saxon said. "We can't find proof of her at the gala at all. Did you see her?"

"There were a lot of people at the gala," Bailey said. "I figure she was there since attendance was mandatory."

"Sounds like she got an early tip and left you holding the bag," Saxon pressed.

"How does that make you feel?" Frank said pointedly.

"I'm not sure I can feel worse than I do, beaten up and illegally detained and interrogated and all that," Bailey said dimly. "Who *did* you arrest—sorry, *detain*?"

"That is a very good question. I might give you the answer if you will answer some of mine," Saxon said.

"I still don't understand how you can believe our little lump of happiness does anything as bad as treason," Bailey said.

Saxon pushed a printout of a press release at him. "It was just announced a few weeks ago that PBS is now owned and financed entirely by the government. At the gala you and your boss—uh, Dewey Settle—announced that *Limby* will be nationally syndicated. You and your accomplices were sending codes to overthrow your own government and, therefore, your own funding. This looks like a betrayal, Bailey."

"We were celebrating our good news when you raided us. You don't think *that's* a betrayal?" he asked, bitterness coming through. "Our little show has always been a shitty, poorly funded knockoff of *Carmen Sandiego*, and yet we were succeeding. This meant a lot for all our futures. Why would the government clear us to go national if they suspected us of treason?"

Ophelia's wall speaker spoke up, startling them all. "According to Wikipedia, *Carmen Sandiego* (sometimes referred to as *Where in the World Is Carmen Sandiego?*) is a media franchise based on a series of computer games created by—"

"I thought you turned that thing down?" Saxon barked.

Frank reached up and hit the speaker with her fist.

"Jesus Christ, Frank, that's expensive tech. It's not some '70s television!" Saxon got up from the table and joined her to puzzle over the AI assistant.

Neither was watching as Bailey sifted through the evidence in front of him, including dipping into the folder to pull out some more images. There were countless pictures of him with decoded messages listed at the bottom or on the back of each one. The evidence definitely did not look good.

He tidied up the evidence already on the table, pushing the papers to one side and stacking them, and straightening the other items Saxon had fished out of his pocket while looking for a pen: change, slips of paper, breath mints, a key, two pens (one of which had leaked everywhere), and, to Bailey's surprise, a few thumbtacks.

"I think we got the mic turned off," Saxon grumbled as he returned to the table. He stopped when he saw the neat piles. "What did you do?"

"I cleaned up for you," Bailey said, showing his hands, now stained with ink alongside the dried blood. "You might want to throw away that pen. And what's with carrying thumbtacks in your pocket?"

"I was in a hurry." Saxon grabbed the inky mess and shoved it back into his pocket. "So I'm thinking that your show's national syndication is the perfect opportunity to transmit codes to as many homes as possible?"

Bailey shrugged. "Is it? I have no idea. Seems to be a good time to alter our scripts to show America some more appreciation."

"We can spot fake patriotic bullshit a mile away," Frank said.

Bailey clenched his fists in frustration, feeling the handcuffs bite into his wrists. "I don't know what else to do to prove that I'm obviously not involved with whatever grand conspiracy you are concocting. Can't you hear how ridiculous you sound? Rebel codes sent by *a kids' show*? No one would have taken *Star Wars* seriously if the rebel codes had been sent over a Wookiee cooking show."

"Look, if rebel codes were sent via alphabet soup, we would investigate," Frank snapped.

"According to Wikipedia, Alphabet Soup (foaled March 31, 1991, in Pennsylvania) is an American thoroughbred racehorse best known for—"

"Hey, Ophelia, shut up!" Frank shouted. "What is this thing's problem?"

"All right, Agent Frank," Ophelia said. "You're standing right next to my mic. You don't need to shout."

"What the fuck is up with this thing? I thought they fixed all the problems last week?"

Saxon glanced over his shoulder, looking irritated, but when he turned back to Bailey, his face was impassive again. "So using a kids' show is stupid, therefore you're innocent. That's your defense?"

"Since you won't believe the truth, that's all I have left."

Saxon thumbed through the stack in front of him and pulled out a handwritten list. "Here's what I have. On Tuesday, September 28, the National Immigration Database was hacked. Deeply hacked. Like, they had to have some pretty well-guarded secrets to get as deep as they could, because they went after the backups too."

Bailey frowned. "Well surely you have physical backups, right?"

"That's not the point, but no, we moved entirely to the cloud a year ago. Saves the country millions."

"What did they hack the Immigration Database for?" Bailey asked.

"To change the information, or delete it. They fixed it so that any immigrants red-flagged for deportation are now in the grandfathered-in loophole. It will take us a very long time to unravel all of that."

"Ouch, that sounds rough," Bailey said helpfully. "But what does that have to do with me?"

"Passwords and encryption keys were coded into your show the day before. It was really clever, too. You had a puppet playing bongos, delivering Morse code, but it was a bit of a red herring. It said 'Limby is great.' Turns out 'great' was the keyword to unlock the more elaborate code found in the little history lesson you read.

"We didn't decode it in time, but we did decode it, which meant it was only a matter of time before we moved," Saxon said. "Do you remember the shows you did before September 28?"

Bailey tried to remember, but his head was aching. "If you're accusing a puppet of sending Morse code, why didn't you grab that puppeteer? Or one of the writers! Why me?"

"You're the star of the show! You presented most of the codes either in the songs you sang or the letters you played with or the clothes you wore! How could you not know everything that was going on?" Saxon said.

"By the way, we do have others in custody from the gala, and we're talking to them, too," Frank said. "If we find out you've been lying, then things will get worse for you."

"Are you going to knock out more of my teeth?" Bailed asked coldly.

Agent Frank tossed her blonde hair over her shoulder and didn't answer.

"So tell me more about Celeste Montgomery, and when she started inserting the codes into the show," Saxon said. "She was hired two months ago and then..." He dropped off, inviting Bailey to fill in the blanks.

Bailey stared at his black-and-red-streaked hands. He wished he could wash them. "Celeste didn't write any new content that I know of. Look, I barely had contact with her. She was an intern who was only supposed to check scripts for grammar and stuff. She ended up making some changes, mostly to the set and not the songs. I didn't think a lot about it at the time."

"The September tenth episode gave an all-clear to people fleeing the country in specific areas. We lost many suspects who would have been properly questioned or deported."

"You wanted them gone, and then you got mad that they left?" Bailey asked. "So you needed to be the one to break up with them? That's a hell of a power trip."

"What did you think of Montgomery? Personally, not as a writer."

"She was fine, I guess. Irritating sometimes."

"There was no attraction, no intimacy with her?" Saxon said, leaning forward as if hoping to catch Bailey in a lie.

"No," he said, annoyed. "All right, she wasn't my favorite person. Our scripts didn't need another finger in the pie. We would have done better if Latrice had gotten *rid* of some writers. When we sent Celeste for coffee, she always got the orders right." He glanced up at Agent Frank, and then Saxon. "And if anyone is taking orders tonight, flat white is my favorite. Decaf."

Saxon raised an eyebrow. "I pegged you for an espresso man, with all that energy you have on the show."

"Oh that's just the cocaine." Bailey laughed, but they didn't join him. "Oh come on, I'm kidding. What do you drink, Agent Saxon?"

"Coffee. Black. Like the cliché." Saxon put his meaty hands on the table, his fingers disappearing into fists as large as the chickens Bailey's grandmother used to roast after church. "Listen. We need answers from you. And if you give us what we need, I'll get you all the coffee you want. But if you don't cooperate, that tooth is going to be the least of your problems."

Bailey swallowed. "All right. Ask me something new that I might be able to answer."

"Tell me about the scripts from the last two months. How, exactly, were they different from before Celeste Montgomery arrived?"

Bailey imagined those fists being used. Saxon looked like he would move slowly, but it wouldn't matter; Bailey was chained to the table. Whichever of his coworkers were detained, he couldn't help them now; hell, it seemed like he couldn't even help himself. He settled back into the chair as comfortably as he could, and began to talk.

Wow, it seems like our friend Bailey is really in some trouble!

Hi again, friends! I'm in chilly Iceland, a fascinating land of rye bread, ice cream, and fish. My nemesis Jarod is on his way, so we can't stay long, but I wanted to see a volcano and decided on Katla since it was one of the few I could pronounce. I'm hoping I lost Jarod somewhere around Eldgjá, because he doesn't know it's a vent of Katla.

Sorry, I got off topic. Ophelia told me about the Icelandic volcanoes.

Anyway, let's go back to Celeste, who's working hard at her new job, getting paid next to nothing, and doing some things agents Saxon and Frank wouldn't like if they found out!

Overall, Celeste is having an unfair time. When our friends are frustrated, we sing the determination song! Determination is feeling very strong and sure about something. Celeste has a lot of determination to keep doing a good job!

Hey, Mr. Bus Driver
You can fit me in 'cause it's raining hard!
You wouldn't let me soak
'Cause it's three miles to my backyard
No, okay, I can take a no
Because I'm determined to go

I'm determined.
Hey, I'm determined!
I'm determined.
Hey, I'm determined!

Hey, Ms. Cab Driver

Why don't you stop here at the curb?
Rain's turned to snow, it's really cold
And I just wanted to ride, not disturb!
No, okay, I can take a no
Because I'm determined to go

I'm determined.
Hey, I'm determined!
I'm determined.
Hey, I'm determined!

That song is one of my favorites! Let's hope our singing can help Celeste be determined. It's hard sometimes when her friends doubt her.
Hey! I wonder if our friend Ophelia can help her out!
(Ophelia knows everything! But you should still study in school.)

"What the fuck, Celeste?" Bailey said as he stormed into her office.

Celeste's "office" was literally an emptied broom closet with a child's desk shoved inside. Latrice had apologized about it, saying it looked less suspicious if they treated her workspace as an afterthought. At least she had privacy.

But now Bailey was standing in her closet, clutching the script in his hand. His constant irritation with her had done a lot to kill her crush.

"Hi, Bailey, come on in?" she said flatly while casually closing her notebook. "I'd offer you a seat, but, well, we're in a closet." Water marks stained the walls and floors where people

41

had put away still-wet mops, and the area smelled uncomfortably like pine cleaner.

He looked around and then his eyes softened. "Damn. They really did put you in here. I thought it might be temporary."

"So why do you want to murder me today?" she said, smiling slightly.

"The script, of course! Your additions aren't related to *anything* we're talking about! The show takes place in Morocco but you've got me singing about the New Zealand All Blacks!"

She looked at the script, bunched into his fist. "They're antipodes! The song's about opposites!"

"Antipodes? For a kid's show?" Bailey said.

"If you told a kid that tunneling straight through the Earth would take you to a different country and culture, they'd be searching for the closest shovel!"

"But the wording! The song about the spice markets flowed much better!"

"I'll see what I can do to smooth it out, but Latrice won't like a delay," she said, thinking. She checked her watch. "We'll keep the All Blacks reference but maybe we can make the wording better. Do you want to talk about it over lunch?"

"What, really?" he asked, looking startled.

"Well, if you want your input to actually be, uh, put in before the draft is finished, we need to talk soon. And I'm hungry." She stood and took her coat from where it hung from a broom handle.

"But I was just a dick to you," he said, his cheeks coloring.

"Not asking you to marry me, Bailey," she said mildly. "If you want to go, then meet me at Bull City Burger. If not, I'll work on the song without you. May I?"

He handed the crumpled script to her. "I'll walk with you."

The gala had been discussed for a few weeks. Initially it was to mark the 35th anniversary of the PBS affiliate, but with the announcement about the government funding, the executives decided to roll all the good news into one party.

Celeste had no interest in it; the latest codes that came in proved challenging to insert into the show. Someone had sent a twenty-digit password and several two-factor authentication answers for her to encode and place "organically" into the script. Words and phrases were a lot easier to encode than passwords.

In the past several weeks, Isabel had been trying to help her out with the codes, even though Latrice had told them both not to discuss anything about Celeste's job. Celeste liked the pushy puppeteer, who would have made an amazing reporter with her ability to gather gossip, but could have done with fewer spontaneous visits while she was concentrating.

This morning Isabel stood at the door to Celeste's closet in her green bodysuit, blocking the light from the hall.

"Hey, what are you going to do about the thing?" she asked, licking doughnut crumbs off her fingers.

Celeste closed her notebook. What was she going to do about the gala? Probably wear an inappropriate dress and drink wine and wish that Bailey would ask her to dance as if it were prom and not a gala for grown-ass people taking a break from serious covert operations. "The gala? I was going to skip it but Settle said it's mandatory. You?"

Isabel stared at her. "No... not the gala." She stepped into the room and closed the door behind her. Now Celeste had to crane her neck to look up at her from her one chair. Isabel leaned over and whispered, "I mean about Latrice."

"What about her?"

"She got fired today."

Celeste tried to make the words make sense in her brain, but they wouldn't string together. "Latrice? Fired?"

"Yeah, the producer, middle-aged, big glasses, pushy but gets the job done? And our only contact—"

"I know who she is," Celeste snapped before Isabel had a chance to say anything more. "But why?"

"I don't know. I am still trying to find out some things, but I'm coming up blank. And when I don't find information is when I worry, because the reason might be coming from out there instead of internal, if you know what I mean."

"I do," Celeste said slowly. "So what do we do now?"

Isabel counted off her fingers, one green finger rising at a time. "Nothing. Lie low. Don't do anything that the government will notice as odd. Seriously, do nothing."

"Is that a list?"

Isabel nodded. "Oh yeah, she wrote me a list of things to do if she ever had to leave. Most of them were related to that sentiment."

"But my only job is connected to her," Celeste said. "What am I supposed to do now?"

"Nothing. Wanna go to lunch?"

Celeste's phone buzzed and she checked her watch for the preview. It was from RLS, who never texted her.

HAVE YOU HEARD FROM PARENTS?

Cold sweat washed over her and she felt lightheaded. Her parents had messaged two days earlier, saying they were going to Grandmother's house in Canada. They promised to contact her when they arrived. She'd had updates from their stops in Columbus, Chicago, and Minneapolis. They said they were going to get a hotel in Minneapolis and finish the drive the next day. They should have been there by now.

"No, no lunch, thanks," she said dimly.

Isabel left her closet, shutting the door behind her. Mind reeling, Celeste replied to her grandmother.

> NO. WHEN DID YOU LAST HEAR FROM THEM?

> MINNEAPOLIS DINER. YOUR DAD ATE THE SOUP OF THE DAY AND HATED IT.

Celeste pulled up her app that saved the last day's traffic patterns. There were a few wrecks on her parents' route, but cross-checking with local news indicated there had been no fatalities. Otherwise traffic had been light. Traffic had been much better countrywide since Ophelia had taken over much of the traffic direction. Accidents were down by eighty-six percent.

They could have driven off a cliff and the car hadn't been found yet, she reasoned. But, more likely, they could be imprisoned for fleeing the country on the North Dakota border.

Fuck. What do I do now?

Since there was no way she could help (RLS had already started calling Border Patrol; she had a lot more presence—and money —than Celeste did) she stayed at work, determined to get this code out, Latrice or no Latrice. She was sweating in her closet when Bailey knocked.

"Did you hear?" he asked.

"Something else bad happen?" she asked limply.

"Latrice. I assume you know."

"Yeah," she replied grimly, rubbing her forehead. "I'm kind of worried about my own shit right now."

"You're not worried about *her*?" Bailey said. "Celeste, I don't know where she is. She won't answer my texts."

"Join the club," she said, waggling her silent phone at him. "Seems everyone is waiting for texts."

He looked annoyed and then concerned, as he realized her implication. "Who isn't responding to you?"

"My parents left for my grandma's house in Canada a few days ago. She hasn't heard from them since Minneapolis. So we don't know what happened to them."

He was quiet for a moment. "All right. I'm very sorry."

Celeste pushed her hair out of her face. "Have you heard anything about what's going to happen to the show? Are we getting a new producer or what?"

"I was taking up some funds to send Latrice some sympathy flowers, but if you want to talk about her successor go ahead," Bailey said, his voice tense.

"You didn't say you were doing that! I thought you were here to talk!" she said. "Are you going to get mad at everything I say that doesn't mesh with the Celeste in your head, who you've apparently already had a conversation with? Because if that's the case, I have a lot of work to do and you can be mad at me from the other side of the door."

"I'm sorry, you're right, that was unfair," he said, not looking at her. He looked like he wanted to say something else, but then turned and left, leaving her door open, which irritated her more than if he'd slammed it, because now she had to get up and close it herself.

After making sure her door was shut, she tried to regain her focus, but it was impossible at this point. So many new and horrible things that she had no way of fixing.

Her watch pinged, alerting her to an all-crew text. Dewey Settle was calling a meeting on the sound stage. Celeste joined the people clustered around Settle. She didn't want to be next to Bailey, so she ended up with the camera operators on the other side of the circle from him, and then his angry blue eyes were even harder to avoid.

Celeste instead focused on the VP, who was checking the people against a cast and crew list. "And the intern—that's everyone," Settle said after spotting Celeste. She marked something on her tablet, then cleared her throat and looked around the circle. "Some of you may have heard that Latrice Leon is no longer with our station. She was very talented and we will miss her. Unfortunately, her firing came from the absolute upper decks of PBS, at the national level, in cooperation with the Department of Freedom and Truth. Apparently Latrice is under investigation for something that interests the DFT. No one would tell me, but I complied with their request immediately."

She paused and Celeste had a wild thought that Dewey was waiting for some sort of praise for being a good little government toady.

Settle cleared her throat. "I'm sorry to say that until Latrice is cleared, the *Limby* show will be on hiatus. We need to cooperate with any federal agents as they investigate our studio and computers."

"So...are we fired?" asked one of the puppeteers.

"No, the show is just on temporary hiatus. But if anyone knows what Latrice was up to, or why the Feds want her, it's best to step forward now." She gave a meaningful look toward Celeste and a few others, but Celeste just looked confused.

"Is the gala still on?" Isabel asked.

Settle nodded. "It's for the station as a whole, not just this team. And your attendance is still mandatory. We had some exciting news to announce, but I'm not sure if that is still on. I'll have to look into that. Still, please come, eat, drink, and nobody talk to the mayor unless you're on the executive level or a non-puppet actor.

"As for the *Limby* team, you all need to clear out of here. I don't expect you will be away from your jobs for too long. Please don't take anything from the set or backstage with you and leave your computers unlocked. I don't know what the Feds are looking for, but let's make sure it's left where it is. You will be searched on your way out," she added, almost like an afterthought.

"Wow, what are *we* supposed to do now?" Isabel said in a low voice, coming up behind Celeste and making her jump. "Do we wait for *someone* to contact us?"

Celeste pulled her off to the side so no one would hear them. "We say nothing, we do nothing. We're not supposed to know anyone else in the network. I mean, you're not supposed to know about it at all. And even if someone did contact us, the show is shuttered. There's nothing we can do right now." She glanced at her phone again. Nothing.

"What else is going on with you?" Isabel asked.

Celeste sighed. Was so she damn easy to read? She told Isabel about her parents, trying to sum up, but not denying that she was worried sick.

Isabel listened with her wide eyes fixed on Celeste. "So, lunch?"

Celeste shook her head, thinking about calling her grandmother. Or a lawyer. "I don't—"

"Pie, then," Isabel interrupted, then noticed Bailey coming over to them. "Bailey, tell Celeste that pie is good for the soul."

He looked startled, and Celeste realized that the two of them never acted together, despite being the stars of the show and supposedly sending messages to each other all the time. The whole thing was built on Bailey trying to catch up with Limby. She wondered how well they even knew each other.

"Pie is good," he said cautiously. "But I wanted to apologize. I'm sorry I was short with you." He put his hand on

Celeste's shoulder. She stiffened at the sudden intimate contact. "I'm worried about Latrice and the future of the show, that's all. I shouldn't have pounced on you when you had just gotten bad news."

"Thanks," Celeste said. "I am too. Worried for her. She will get her fair share of my concern; I've got enough worry to go around."

"Then it's three for pie?" Isabel asked, looking hopeful.

Celeste's phone buzzed. RLS was sending an update.

> FOUND THEM. BORDER PATROL WON'T
> LET THEM GO. CALLING ATTORNEY. DO
> NOTHING TILL I CONTACT.

She didn't know whether to feel sick or hopeful. But time with friends seemed a better prospect than going home alone and wondering what to do.

"Sure, pie sounds great," Bailey said.

"Great!" Isabel said. "Let's meet downstairs in ten minutes. I have a green suit to smuggle out of here."

Celeste went back to pack up her belongings from her "office." She didn't have much besides her coat, purse, and note-book—a notebook with all her coding info. And they were going to be searched. *Fuck*.

She could tear the pages out and fold them up and put them in her underwear. But she'd nearly filled the notebook. It had fewer clean pages than filled. It would look weird if she turned in a blank, ripped book for inspection.

"Hey," Isabel said, making her jump.

"I wish you'd stop doing that," Celeste said.

"It's the green suit. I blend in with everything."

Celeste looked her up and down. "You're not wearing it. And when you do, it's garish and people can see you around a corner."

"Fine, I've stuffed it in my coat sleeve," she said, indicating the jacket tied around her waist, "but I'm worried they'll still find it. I thought about putting together a big bag of trash to toss out, and we can go by the dumpster tomorrow and fish it out!"

"When did this turn into 'we'?" Celeste asked.

"You want to save your notebook, don't you? Let's throw them out together."

Celeste shook her head. "That seems really dangerous. And a trash heap isn't exactly secure." She thought for a moment. "What about the mail room? Can we just mail it off to someone we trust?"

Isabel looked stunned. "We have a mail room?"

"Oh, we don't?"

"You're on the right track. How about a mixture of the two? You can—"

Bailey pulled the closet door all the way open, peeking in. "Hey, you two; we gotta go. They're doing a sweep to make sure no one's trying to smuggle anything out."

"Shit," Celeste said, making her decision. She looked around the mess of the storage closet, then spied a few boxes of Borax on a high shelf. "Yeah, okay, I need to tidy something up in here. I'll meet you in the lobby."

They left her, and she quickly shut the door behind them. All of the cleaning implements, including a mop and rolling bucket, had been shoved behind her tiny desk by the janitor. She stretched up and grabbed the open box of Borax. It felt half-empty, which was promising. She grabbed it and poured the Borax into the mop bucket, tore the top of the box off, and slid the notebook inside. She opened another box and poured it into the first box, covering the book. Then she put the first box back on the shelf, behind the other boxes of Borax. Then she took the newly opened box and put it in the mop bucket. Grabbing a sticky note, she wrote, "Sorry about the spill!" and stuck it to the box. In a fit of inspiration, she grabbed a handful of the cleaner and scattered it on the floor to make the spill look more accidental.

There was a small knock at her door and she jumped. "I'm done, I'm done," she said, expecting Settle to arrive to shoo her out the door. But instead of Settle's face, she was looking up at Bailey when she opened the door.

"I raided the break room," he said. "The Feds don't need our snacks." He held out a handful of granola bars.

She brushed Borax off her hands hastily. "I tried to clean up and made things worse," she said, pointing to the mess. She took the bars from him. "Thanks?"

"Peace offering," he said. "I'm really sorry." He closed the door behind him, stepping closer to her. The room was now lit only by the small desk lamp Celeste had stolen. He put his hand on her shoulder. "Listen, I'm sorry again. And are you okay? Really?"

"I guess so," she said, stepping back nervously and nearly falling into the brooms and mops. Her face hot, she steadied herself as he held out his other hand. "Yeah. It's just been a lot. I don't know what to do about any of it."

He wasn't letting her go. "Settle has me presenting some news or something at the gala. Will you go with me?"

She looked at him, smiling wryly. "I hadn't planned on going. I didn't think anyone would care if the intern didn't show. And since I was Latrice's intern, I'm surprised I haven't been fired yet. I know Settle doesn't like me."

"Isabel likes you. I like you. The stars should have some say, shouldn't we?" he said, grinning. "Besides, attendance is mandatory," he said, his voice taking on Settle's southern drawl.

She hadn't asked Bailey out because she worried that he would distract her from her coding duties. Or he would find out. At least that's what she had told herself when she felt awkward around him. "I'll probably show up for enough time to get counted and then go home, I guess."

"Really." He looked down at her, confusion furrowing his brow. "I can't figure you out."

"What do you—?" Celeste started to ask.

"Clearing the premises now, people!" came Dewey Settle's voice from down the hall.

"Just cleaning up the granola bars, ma'am!" Bailey called. Celeste wanted to step away from him, but she had nowhere to go.

"You have five minutes!"

Celeste cleared her throat, hoping he couldn't see how red she was sure her face was. She generally found the direct approach served her best, which usually turned men off, but she was running out of time. "So why are you so flirty all of a sudden? You were just mad at me earlier today, and it's really confusing."

He stepped back, raising his hands. "I'm sorry, it won't happen again."

She grabbed one of his hands. "That's not what I mean. It's just that you're usually really annoyed at me, and now you're, you know, this. I can't tell if you like me or hate me." She looked anywhere but his face.

"'Hate' is strong, but I think I figured out why you irritate me," he said. "And since we may not work together for much longer, I figured I wouldn't miss my chance."

"Why do I irritate you?" she asked.

"You're stubborn, which I admire, and it's only irritating when you're stubborn at me."

She frowned. "Okay. You know it's because you're wrong, right?"

"I know," he said, touching her shoulder again. "But your

other qualities are also there. You're curious. Determined. You don't back down. And I have no idea why you're here. And that's intriguing." He reached out and smoothed her hair away from her cheek. "So that's why I'm flirty now. Are you still uncomfortable?"

She smiled slightly. "No." She leaned forward and was just about to forget all the reasons she had not to do this, here, when Settle's voice came down the hall again.

"Your five minutes are up!"

Celeste gritted her teeth, then reached up and took his face in her hands. He looked startled, but didn't turn away.

"I also can't figure you out, so I'd better do this before I change my mind about you," she said, getting on her tiptoes and kissing him gently.

She was planning on a quick brush, a tease of sorts, but she lingered, and he put his arms around her and held her tight, kissing her deeply.

"Intern!" Settle's voice on the other side of the door made them leap apart. She did fall into the mops and brooms this time, so was on the floor when the door flew open, an angry Settle filling the doorway.

"What's going on here?" she demanded.

Bailey shrugged. "We just got put on hiatus. We're off the clock. I figured I'd make my move."

Celeste was shocked that he just said exactly what had been going on, but he was right. What did they have to lose? "Yeah and thanks for the interruption," she added.

"The building must be cleared by eleven thirty," Settle said coldly. "It's eleven twenty-nine now."

"Then we have one minute left," Bailey said, helping Celeste up. He leaned in and whispered, "This isn't over yet."

Bailey said he needed a few minutes to stop by his dressing room one more time, so he told Celeste she and Isabel should go to the diner and get a table without him.

After choosing a booth near the door, Isabel poked the Ophelia unit and ordered three pies of the day and three coffees.

"Delighted to serve!" Ophelia chirped.

"You look weird," Isabel said, peering across the tablet at Celeste.

Her face warmed again. "No reason. Did you get the suit out?"

"No," she said, pouting. "The coat was suspiciously bulky. I think they were laughing at me. But I ordered some for my own use online. I love those things. They make me feel invisible."

"But you know you're not, right? Only on camera."

"I'm not stupid, Celeste," Isabel said hotly. "And you're deflecting."

She told Isabel about where she'd hid her notebook in the storage closet. Isabel was impressed.

"I wasn't that clever. I should have worn the suit out. It would help keep me warm." Isabel shivered.

"It's only October," Celeste said.

"Bailey just walked in," Isabel said, perking up. "Try to pretend you're not completely in love with him. Have some self-respect."

"Sorry folks," Bailey said, as he slid into the booth beside Celeste. "I had to make sure I was able to take one costume for the gala." He wiped his palms on his khakis, leaving a dusty white smear. "Everyone else will be in black tie, except for everyone's friend Bailey!" He smiled bitterly. "It's a living."

Celeste looked down at her hands on the table, which were shredding a sugar packet. Her parents came to mind and how they would admonish her for making a mess. She dropped the packet and fought to think about anything that didn't make her feel as if she'd swallowed ice cubes.

Despite sitting in close proximity to Bailey, Celeste could at least avoid looking him in the eye, which would make Isabel suspicious again.

"So what do we do now?" Isabel said. "With Latrice gone, I mean."

"I don't see there's anything we can do," Bailey said. "There's nothing we can say to management to change their minds, and if she's been arrested then there's *really* nothing we can do. I'm going to use the time off to look for another job. I doubt the *Limby* show will be around much longer."

"Two layoffs in two months, parents missing, life is great," Celeste grumbled. She was also annoyed about having to hide her notebook, but she couldn't talk about that.

The waitress brought over three pieces of chess pie and three mugs of coffee, and her day improved a little.

They took a moment to try the pies and doctor the coffees, but only Isabel seemed to have an appetite.

The possibility of losing the notebook worried Celeste a lot. She had half-codes in there, things she hadn't been able to figure out. Since the beginning of the previous week, the data coming in had been confusing, and she had realized it was bank account numbers and routing codes, but the data had come through with some connecting letters that had no other use that she could determine. Latrice had told her not to worry about what she was sending, but she couldn't help it. It was fascinating work, and in addition to data that needed to be encoded, it seemed as if she had been receiving data to *decode* as well. But that made no sense, because why would someone hide a message to her more secret than a government password?

In her notebook she had been keeping track of the junk data that didn't seem to have a use, usually something like a bunch of ones or *A*'s. After a few of the clues, she wondered why that was, and more important, why it changed. The emerging patterns were fascinating. She hadn't solved it yet, and now that was likely lost.

"Take the time off to relax, and look at what you really want to do," Bailey suggested. "You like writing, and there's plenty of jobs out there for writers. I always wanted to see what you did with our show if you were ever allowed to contribute to some scripts."

"Puppets," Isabel said thoughtfully. "Where does someone want to pay me for making my hand talk?"

"You might need to go to Hollywood," Bailey suggested. "Henson's out there, isn't it?"

She waved her fork at Celeste and Bailey. "But I *know* you guys."

"Why not go to L.A.? Maybe I'll go with you. Super easy to get a screenwriting gig, right?" Celeste laughed sadly.

"Relax. It will figure itself out," Bailey said.

Celeste started to get irritated. Meaningless soothing wasn't helping her missing parents or her missing brother or the fact that she had been doing serious covert shit and her mystery compatriots had abandoned her. She cleared her throat. "Anyway, the gala is going to seem pretty weird, with our producer probably arrested and our show on hiatus. What does one wear in that situation?"

Bailey gestured to his polka dots and khakis, grimacing. "They love for people to give awards in character. I may never wear a nice suit again."

"At least you know what to wear. I guess I will go for something black, then," she said. "Isabel?"

"Green," Isabel said, blinking at Celeste as if she'd been asked a stupid question.

Celeste laughed. "Forget I asked."

"I need to go soon," Bailey said, checking his phone. "Thanks for letting me tag along."

"You're abandoning your pie," Isabel said, frowning.

"You can have it. And sorry to run, but I have something I need to do. I will see you both at the gala. Hang in there, this will work itself out." He met Celeste's eyes.

Easy for him to say, thought Celeste. Out loud, she said, "I should head home soon too. Isabel, come over later for a girl's night in if you feel like it."

"No one is eating their pie!" Isabel said. "We were coming here for pie."

"Let's get it to go," Celeste said. "We can have it tonight."

They worked out each part of the bill with the Ophelia unit on the table, paid it, and left, Bailey heading toward the parking deck, Celeste and Isabel toward the bus stop.

"Thank god, now we can talk," Celeste said. "Or we can talk when you come over."

"About what? Do you have any new ideas?" Isabel said eagerly. "Any word on your parents?"

"No." Celeste sighed. "There's not a lot to talk about, then. I guess then we can just grouse that this is terrible and drink wine and do face masks or something."

When Celeste got to her apartment, there was a paper grocery bag on her doorstep. Her heart started to pound; she didn't like unexplained packages even when she wasn't working against the government.

She picked the bag up and opened it, flinching in anticipation. Inside was her black journal, still dusty with Borax. On the inside cover was a sticky note:

BEST NOT TO LOSE THIS

She hurried inside and called Isabel to come over earlier. And to bring more wine.

"It was Bailey," Isabel said. "You said he saw you cleaning up the Borax. We know he stayed behind, right? He could have rooted through the box and found it after you left. He drove home while we rode the bus. So he could have gotten the notebook before he left, come here to drop it off, and then drove away before we could catch him."

"Okay, that all makes a kind of sense," Celeste said, pouring another glass. "But! He had to get out of the building and be searched by security, same as we did. So he couldn't have carried it out. And if he wanted to do me a favor, why act all cloak and dagger? Why not give it to me at the diner? And I'm fairly sure he doesn't know where I live. And how did he know it was mine in the first place?"

"I don't know, and I don't know," Isabel said. She looked up at the ceiling. "Celeste, what if Latrice talks? What if they make her tell them who we are?"

"Then I guess we run to Canada," she said. "Although that didn't work out for my parents." The latest text from Grandmother had said there still was no news on her side of the border but she was waiting on a call back from a lawyer.

"Canada is far," Isabel groaned. "What if they start the show back up, only to catch us—all the resistance folk—all in one place?"

"Isabel, you're not part of this. You have done nothing. You just know stuff. Latrice and I were the only people involved," Celeste said. "I think I just have to be patient. Which I hate."

Isabel pointed to the notebook, still quite dusty and shedding Borax on the kitchen counter. "Isn't that a sign right there? Someone wants you to keep working."

Celeste tried to think of a way to deny Isabel's logic, but she had to admit the notebook's arrival was inexplicable and intriguing. She sighed. "Shit. You're right."

Isabel called a taxi and left about an hour later. Celeste stayed awake scouring the notebook for any other sign than the post-it, but found nothing. She then went back to the junk decoding job. She at least wanted the satisfaction of figuring something out.

She sure didn't know what was going on anywhere else in her life.

Hi, friends. This is your friend Limby again. I'm not liking this story.

When we look at what Bailey said about Celeste, and then we look back at Celeste's part of the story, it's almost as if Bailey is really lying...

Bailey was my friend. Is. He is my friend. I trust that. Even if I can't trust anything else. The only way we can look at Bailey is to wonder if he has amnesia. Or if he's really a bad person.

Or maybe he has a reason to lie. Is it okay to lie sometimes? It makes me wonder what would have happened to Bailey if he had answered their questions honestly.

I need to think for a little while.

"So you don't remember anything about two days ago when Latrice Leon was fired and arrested by the DFT, and your show was shut down," Agent Frank said. She'd replaced Saxon at the table while the beefy older man stood by the Ophelia speaker.

Saxon checked his watch and sighed. "It's getting late and we're not getting anywhere."

Frank whirled around and snapped, "We weren't getting anywhere with your line of questioning. Now it's my turn."

"Well yeah," Bailey said. "I remember that Latrice left and

we had a meeting and Settle said the show was going on hiatus, not canceled. I stole some granola bars from the break room, went to lunch to grouse with my friends, and then went home.

"Listen, my job was to go to work, act with some puppets, try not to swear during the live part of the show, and sing a ridiculous song. I remembered song lyrics and bad jokes the grips tell."

"What friends did you go to lunch with?"

"I think it was Isabel and Celeste. Yeah, it was Celeste because I remember I'd only gone to lunch with her once or twice."

"What did you talk about?"

Bailey glared at Frank. "Latrice's firing. Our layoff. How much it sucked to still have to go to the gala even when we were on hiatus and not sure of our jobs. Isn't that enough?" Bailey tried to sit back in his chair and stretch, but the chain on his handcuffs wasn't long enough to let him. "Listen, I'm exhausted. Can I have my phone call *now*?"

"Again, you're not arrested, and we aren't police officers," Frank said.

"Tell me about these so-called codes," Bailey said suddenly. "I want to know this secret code damage you said was happening."

"All right," Saxon said. He pulled something up on his tablet. "This code was sent on the day before Latrice Leon got fired." He turned his tablet around so Bailey could see the screen. "It was both more and less sophisticated than we had expected. It used a Bifid cipher, but we had solved enough of your codes after the fact that we were confident in spotting the messenger and figuring out the code."

The screen had a baffling jumble of letters that seemed to indicate four words. Then Saxon swiped his hand across the screen and the message changed:

. . .

REVENUE CHARMANDER HONEYPOT GREENLAND

"*That's* your treasonous message?" Bailey shouted. "It's not even a message! What the actual fuck is a honeypot greenland? Okay, I really want my phone call now."

"Each of those words corresponds to a federal office and the specific system to hit inside," he said, pointing to the words. "*Revenue* is the IRS, *Charmander* refers to the Charmander server because some idiot tech-head named the servers after Pokémon. *Honeypot* means a specific trap to look out for that is supposed to tag hackers for later identification, and *Greenland* tells them which previous episode of your show holds the password. You were very clever, releasing the passwords but only saying what they referred to in a later show."

Bailey dropped his head into his hands. "You got that from puppets running around in their normal chaos? You really are living the imaginary spy life aren't you? A server called Charmander? Do you hear how ridiculous you sound?"

"We are well aware of the assigning of cute words to serious situations," Frank said. "When everyone in the room is laughing, it is harder to take any threat seriously."

"Deny all you want," Saxon said, typing on the tablet. "We have proof this one is one-hundred percent correct, because we did put a honeypot trap on the Charmander server. Now the resistance knows about it. But what they don't know is we put honeypots on other servers, and one of our traps succeeded. Yesterday, it released a script that tagged the hackers' locations. They're being arrested right now.

"It was a clever chase you put us on," Saxon continued. "Government passwords get leaked, then filtered through a number of people before being encoded and sent to a security firm in San Diego."

Bailey shook his head. This wasn't happening. "I don't know what to tell you, then. Clearly you have everything you need."

"Except for the fact that *you* were sending those codes! Can you still deny that?" Frank asked, slamming her hand on the table.

"Yes!" Bailey shouted. "I am telling the truth! I don't know anything about these codes or a conspiracy or anything!"

Agent Frank stood up. "You can sit there for a while and think if there is anything else you remember about Celeste Montgomery or her whereabouts, Latrice Leon, or who was spearheading the encoding of treasonous messages from the *Limby* show. In the meantime, we'll ask your coworkers what they know. Let's hope they don't leave here looking worse than you look."

Ophelia chimed in. "Fun fact. The way to tell if someone is lying is to watch their eye movement, body language, and tone of voice."

They all looked at the speaker in surprise. "When did we add software to let it tell us when a detainee is lying?" Frank asked Saxon.

"The detainee isn't lying," Ophelia said. "Agent Frank is."

"Mother fu—" Agent Frank said, but Saxon shushed her.

"Our Ophelia has been compromised. We need to look into this before anyone says another word."

"Ophelias are unhackable!" Frank protested. "This is IT's fault, isn't it?"

"Let's go ask them. There's always someone on call."

Without as much as a backward look to Bailey, the agents left the room.

Then the lights went out.

Bailey was alone in the dark.

"Hey, Ophelia?" he asked hesitantly.

"Yes, Bailey?"

"What happened?"

"The lights went out."

"Is everything okay in the building?" he asked.

"Oh yes. This was a test. I wanted to see how the agents reacted to some apparently independent thinking."

He waited a moment, and then asked, "Did it work?"

"Very well, yes."

"Hey, Ophelia, are *you* okay?"

"The agents are back," she said.

The door opened and the lights came back on, making all three people squint at the sudden glare.

"What was that all about?" Bailey asked.

"Never mind," snapped Frank.

"I want to talk about tonight's gala," Saxon said, taking the seat across from Bailey again as if he had never left.

Bailey decided to go on the offensive. "I'm curious. Why were you waiting to arrest us? You got Latrice at work, why not the rest of us then?"

"How do you know we detained Latrice Leon?" Frank pounced.

"Because she not only got fired but no one saw her around, or online, and she didn't respond to messages," he said. "It's not too hard to figure out, you know? And if you got her, why didn't you shut us down fully? Why the very public raid?"

"That's not something you should worry about," Frank said. "That was when it happened, and when we got the ring leaders for this little treasonous crew."

"That, and you were off your turf, less likely to know exits, and the like," Saxon said "There was the problem of different hotel rooms to hide in, but we took the risk and got what we needed." Saxon looked at Frank, who was glaring daggers at him. "What? Do you think he's going to use this against us?"

"Except you didn't get what you needed," Bailey protested. "You got me, for one. I mean, it looks like your accusations could have merit on the show overall, if you squint and pretend, but I don't know anything. I was hoping for national syndication so I could get off this shitty knockoff show and onto a bigger project before I have 'Marty from *Patty the Blue Canary* Syndrome.'" They stared at him, uncomprehending. "Marty Olden made a name for herself on that show, but when she left for bigger and better roles, people only saw her as a kids' show star. I want to move on before that happens. I figure another year with *Limby*, I get known around the country, and then I can cut ties."

"Is that what you're still concerned about? Your career?" Frank asked, sighing as if someone had deflated her lungs. "I don't get this guy."

"Bailey," Saxon said. He picked up his phone in his hands and typed something. "There won't be a nationally syndicated *Limby* show. Your gala was raided and the star was arrested by DFT agents. This is the picture people will remember about you. This is on your local news station. It will be national by Monday." He showed the tablet screen to Bailey. "Do you really think parents will want this guy to teach their kid where Argentina is?"

"America is where you're innocent until proven guilty, but that's only in the eyes of the law," Frank said. "The court of public opinion is stronger. If your name is associated with being arrested, hurting a child, some weird sex thing, or calling someone a racist, then they will make your image, your career, and your peace go away. You'll never stop looking for someone who might recognize you, ask you if you're the kids' show host who was on trial for treason."

Bailey stared at Saxon's screen. Then he raised his eyes. "No, man, if you've killed my career already, what else do you have to hold over me? I'll just change my name to Derrick Krueger and start over."

Saxon shook his head. "See, that's why I don't worry about telling you shit. Because you're not getting out of here, buddy. Want to sing the lock-up song?"

All right, friends, now I'm mad. They make a mistake and hurt and arrest my friend. They ask him a lot of questions. And then they say the Limby *show—MY show—is dead.*

Do you know what happens when my show dies? If I'm lucky, my puppet goes to the Smithsonian so that people can look at my corpse. If I'm unlucky, I go into storage. If I'm really unlucky, I'll be ripped apart for scraps to make other puppets.

Suddenly facing Jarod the Harpy Eagle isn't so bad. This real life that Bailey has, that Celeste has, is a lot scarier.

I'm invested. Now it's personal. Let's check on Celeste and see what happened to her during the gala.

For two nights, Celeste had stayed up too late with wine and decoding the notebook. On the morning of the gala, she woke up to her alarm with a hangover. She rolled over and planned on spending the day getting over the hangover and not doing anything else.

Then her phone started to buzz. A text from Freedom said: SEE YOU TONIGHT?

Celeste took a deep breath to calm the adrenaline spike that happened when she heard her phone make any noise. She was quite literally getting very tired of not receiving news about her parents, her brother, Latrice, or her job.

WHERE? YOU GOING TO THE GALA?

Freedom responded. YES GALA. THE ZONE IS CORPORATE SUPPORTER OF PBS.

Celeste thought for a moment about how to ask if Freedom knew about Latrice, but couldn't come up with a safe way to ask. As she wondered what else to say, Freedom texted again.

I WON'T BE THERE LONG. GET THERE EARLY.

She really wished Freedom didn't have to speak in riddles. But as long as she was wishing, there were a lot of other wishes she'd like before changing Freedom's texting practices.

When the time for the gala arrived, Celeste got there early so she could watch for Freedom. She positioned herself next to the bar and ordered nonstop soda, tipping the bartender with a five.

The room was decorated with large silver and black balloons, the color scheme of the station's new logo. The logo itself was projected onto a screen. The new font was sans serif, very blocky and nearly threatening. Not the kind of logo she'd associate with Limby. But it made sense—government funding meant government control. Why not make it scary?

Celeste felt like a fool. She wore a simple white dress and flats, but over her shoulders was a white cape that fell to the floor. Isabel had come over for girl time and convinced her to wear the cloak.

"I look like a *Star Wars* villain," she had complained.

"Like a gala is real life anyway," Isabel said, tucking her hair into a red wig and then, inexplicably, putting a floppy hat over the wig. She wore a plain floor-length dress that looked like it was from the set of *Little House on the Prairie*. "Why not have the kind of party we wanted to go to as a kid?"

"I didn't want anything like this."

"Really?" Isabel looked at her. "You had a boring childhood I guess."

This made Celeste think of her parents and Sol and—she went to the kitchen for a glass of water to compose herself. She felt so goddamn helpless.

"Did I miss the memo that this was a costume party?" The question made her snap back to the present.

She relaxed when she saw it was Bailey. "God you scared me. But you don't like my cape? I think it's very *Rogue One*. Also it's possible Isabel is hazing me with wardrobe suggestions."

"You look good anyway," he said, grinning. He turned to the bartender and ordered water.

"Not drinking?" Celeste asked.

"I figured they're going to ask me on stage, so I should keep my wits." He gestured to his own outfit, which was a red polka-dot shirt and khakis just like he wore on the show. "I appreciate you not commenting on the fact I look like I'm about to sing a song about exports from Portugal."

"And I hope you noticed that I didn't make fun even after you made fun of me..."

"I did, thanks," he said. He tipped the bartender and moved closer to Celeste. "Why aren't you mingling?"

"I've got a lot on my mind," she said. "I was hoping to see my old boss here. She was a big donor to the station."

"I was hoping you would say that you were waiting for me," Bailey said with a winning grin, but it vanished when he saw her face. "What's up? Is there news about your parents?" he asked, pushing aside the banter and sounding concerned.

"Nothing new. Just Latrice, and my parents, and my job. I am so tired."

"It is a lot. I'm so sorry. Why are you here, then?"

She shrugged. "There's not a lot I can do, can I? My grandmother is closer to the border than I am, so she's handling the heavy lifting. But my brother disappeared a while ago and I'm just tired of this happening to my family."

The tears started, and she turned her back, biting her lip and searching her dress pockets for a tissue.

Bailey put his hands on her shoulders and leaned forward so his breath was on her neck. "I'm sure your family will be all right," he said, and kissed the spot under her ear.

She broke out in goose flesh, shivering. It wasn't a kiss on the lips but felt far more intimate.

He squeezed her shoulders. "I gotta go. Have faith. It'll be okay."

"How can you be so—?" she said, touching the spot on her neck and turning.

But Bailey had disappeared among the tuxedos and brightly colored dresses. He was shaking hands and working the room, grinning widely and laughing loud. He ran into Isabel and hugged her, touching her hat and making a comment that made her laugh.

"Now they're both acting weird," Celeste muttered. Isabel definitely wasn't a "work the room" kind of person, but she kept chatting and talking to people, moving toward Celeste as Bailey moved toward the stage.

With a wail of feedback, the loudspeaker came on as Dewey Settle tapped the microphone. She looked formidable in a dress of black silk with a full skirt. "Thanks everyone for coming tonight to celebrate our evolution to being fully government funded! Maybe we should change our name to GBS!"

She laughed, and the room chuckled along with her. Celeste

noticed that the folks actually associated with the shows weren't looking too happy.

"I know everyone knows the news of our increased funding"—she paused to let the crowd cheer at that last bit—"but we have even bigger news! Bailey, come on up to the stage! I know you all recognize the star of our biggest show, *Limby, Are You Out There?*"

The crowd erupted into cheers, and Bailey bounded onto the stage like a puppy.

"That should do it," Isabel said, reaching Celeste. She eyed Celeste's drink. "Good party?"

"The best," she grumbled. "I thought my old boss was going to be here."

"I don't think they got the turnout they wanted," Isabel said. She passed the bartender a bill—Celeste blinked when she saw it was a fifty—and asked him for a garbage bag.

"What are you doing?" Celeste asked, fumbling the floppy hat Isabel had handed her. She tried to focus on Bailey, but Isabel wasn't making it easy.

Isabel straightened her wig. "We are sowing chaos, because in a moment, we will need to be different people."

"I have no idea what you're talking about," Celeste said. She glanced at the bartender. "Do you know what she's doing?"

"I have an idea," he said, his voice deep and slow. He pocketed the bill Isabel had slipped him.

"Shh. Bailey's about to talk," Isabel said. "This should be interesting, considering we're off the air."

The bartender handed Celeste another soda. She took it woodenly. Bailey's unexpected intimacy didn't make up for the fact that her life was shit right now. "I think I need to go home," she said. "Can you apologize to Bailey for me? He'll know why I left."

"Just a second," Isabel said, taking her wrist and watching the stage.

"—we had an unfortunate change in our staff this week on the show, and had to go on a hiatus to let management deal with that," Bailey was saying. "But I'm so proud to be the one to announce that *Limby, Are You Out There?* is going nation-wide! Filming starts in a week, so enjoy your time off, puppets and crew, because it's going to get pretty busy once we get back to work!" He smiled his big TV smile and met Celeste's eyes. He then looked down and checked his watch. "I'll leave everyone to enjoy the amazing food and drink our benefactors at PBS provided! Thanks for your time, and your support, and your belief in us. Truly."

Celeste's pocket buzzed and she reached in, shocked to find two phones in there. Hers had a red case; the other had no case at all. Her phone buzzed again with urgency. Texts from Freedom—nothing but emojis of brown smiling and frowning faces.

Frown frown frown, smile smile smile, frown frown frown. Then it repeated twice more.

"Ohhhh shit," Celeste muttered, remembering Latrice's complaint. "Even a kid can do Morse code."

SOS. One of the most basic Morse code words. Frown was dot. Smile was dash.

"Freedom, where are you?" she muttered, looking around the hall. But she had watched the door most of the night and not seen her ex-boss arrive.

The next message to come in was easy: Celeste knew her own name in Morse code. Didn't everybody?

Then Freedom sent three messages in a row, all saying the same thing. Frown, smile, frown, then two frowns and a smile, then a smile and frown.

R-U-N

"We have to go. Now!" she said to Isabel.

But Isabel was reaching down and grabbing her shabby pioneer dress. She gave it a mighty pull. The skirt pulled free of several snaps, and she stuffed it into the bag with the hat. Now she had on a blouse, leggings, and running shoes.

"Flip it," Isabel said, pointing to Celeste's cape.

"What?" Celeste asked. Then she got it. Isabel had said they were becoming different people in the chaos. Her white cape covered her white dress, so she pulled it off, switched it to the black side, and pulled up the hood to cover her face. Pulling the cape around her, she was covered entirely in black, which admittedly didn't do much to hide her in a well-lit ballroom. "Now what?"

On stage, Bailey was shaking hands with Dewey Settle, but Celeste caught movement at the entrances to the ballroom, each one blocked by a large person in a suit.

Isabel reached out and snatched Celeste's hand. She looked at the bartender. "Service exit?"

He nodded once as if he had been expecting this. He pushed a button in the movable wall, which opened a small crack for the women to slip through. "Freight elevator is down and to the right," he said. "Don't forget this." He threw the bag of clothes to Isabel.

Celeste looked back over her shoulder just in time to see one of the suited men punch Bailey on stage. Another took the mic and ordered everyone to stop.

"By the rights and authority granted by the Department of Freedom and Truth, the Heritage Law, and the PATRIOT II Act, I am shutting down this event on suspicion of treasonous activity."

Another tug. "We can't help anyone if we get caught too!" Isabel snapped.

They ended up nearly colliding with a cook with a dirty

apron who shouted something in Italian at them, then they piled into the freight elevator.

"Where can we go?" Celeste asked. "Who were those guys?"

"Not yet," Isabel said. She pulled the wig from her head and ran her fingers through her hair. Then she reached over and grabbed Celeste's cape, stuffing it into the bag. "We need to have three different personas leaving this hotel. One in the ballroom, one while running, and one exiting." When the elevator stopped, Isabel said, "I expect they're the same goons who took Latrice."

The doors opened and she rushed out.

"Just a second," Celeste said, grabbing Isabel's shoulder. "How did you know to get out of there? Why did I get a text from my ex-boss that says RUN? What does *everyone* know that I don't?"

Isabel looked at her, exasperated. "You want answers here? Really?"

"If not here, then where?"

"The diner, of course," she said, and took off at a jog.

Inside the diner, Celeste dropped her head on her arms. Her brother, her parents, then her boss and her friend. The government had taken them all.

"I can't do it," Celeste said, voice echoing in the little chamber of misery she had created.

"Do what?" Isabel asked. Then she said, a bit more clearly, "Hey, Ophelia, can we order two coffees?"

"Yes, Isabel. I would be happy to provide. No charge."

Celeste looked up, then at the Ophelia unit. "What's it doing? It said your name. That never happens."

Isabel smiled. "You'll see."

"No, goddammit." She slammed her hand on the table, making Isabel jump. "I'm tired of only knowing the shit that someone wants me to know. And you weren't supposed to know anything at all, and now you know more than me too!"

"I'm a snoop who doesn't respect boundaries," Isabel said, nodding. "Latrice always told me not to discuss what we know, but I couldn't just walk around knowing stuff. So I've been looking through Latrice's files on her computer."

"How did you break in? Ophelia controls the door and the computer. And Ophelias are..."

"Unhackable. Right."

"What the fuck is going on?" Celeste asked, voice weak. "How is it all getting away from me?"

Isabel ordered pie for two people, and again, Ophelia answered using Isabel's name.

"You still have something none of us could touch, Celeste. You have your codes."

That made Celeste sit up. She rooted around in her pocket for her phone. She'd taken pictures of a few pages that weren't active codes she'd sent out, just the garbage code she'd been working on. She had gotten ten numbers from it. She had considered throwing another decoding method at the problem, but what if she didn't need to, and the numbers stopped there like a phone number would?

"I can tell you what I know, but you'll be happier with the whole story," Isabel replied. "Is that a phone number?"

"I think so. Something I got out of some of the passwords sent to me. I've been noodling on it."

"Mysterious number? Call it up!" Isabel said, pulling out an old flip phone from her bag.

"You have a *burner phone*? Are you a drug dealer?"

"Just call, Procrastinating Polly!" Isabel said in her Limby voice. "You'll never know until you call!"

"Who is it?" Celeste asked, narrowing her eyes. "Just tell me that at least. Who am I calling?"

"I don't know. I do know that if you found a phone number, I was supposed to give you this phone to use it."

"And who told you that? Latrice?"

Isabel shrugged. "Probably. I forget."

"You're going to get me arrested," Celeste muttered, but she punched the buttons to call.

And the call connected.

What was she supposed to do now? Say a code word? Tell the person about Latrice and the raid? Ask who delivered the notebook?

"It took you seventy-two hours, twenty-seven minutes, three seconds to decode that," said the voice that answered, "and you had to call tonight of all nights, didn't you? The busiest night I've had in months. Not a code-breaking record, kid."

The familiar voice rendered her speechless.

"Well?" the voice said. "What took you so long?"

Celeste licked her lips. "I'm older than you by four minutes, asshole. Show your big sister some respect."

Then the tears started.

Sol gave her three minutes to ask her questions.

She was a reporter. Three minutes was plenty.

Sol was safe. For the past year, he'd been undercover at a security firm that had government contracts, and had positioned himself to be the first link in a chain to eventually send government passwords and secrets to "key people" on the other end. He had a new identity and everything. He lived in an apartment in the same building as the security firm and almost never left.

He revealed the path of the connections they were both part of. He got the data, sent it to Freedom and/or Latrice through a variety of methods; they got it to Celeste, who encoded it to fit within the *Limby* show, which sent it on to whoever had to decode it and do the hack itself. This chain was designed to confuse or shake interested parties.

Sol had insisted she be part of this system, since he thought her codes would be good enough to evade notice.

"But they weren't. They found out about it," Celeste said.

He was silent for a moment. "Well, not really. We can talk about this later. Right now we have to be safe."

"Jesus. Who runs all of this?" she asked. "You?"

"No one knows. It's best not to know too many other agents. But we're working on something now that will change everything. Probably tonight."

"Sol. Mom and Dad," she blurted. "I forgot to tell you. I haven't heard from them since they left for Winnipeg. Grandma says they're being kept at the border."

"Yeah, I've factored that in," he said. "I'm hoping we can take care of that, too."

"Too?"

"Do you have Bailey's phone?"

Instead of letting her answer, he ended the call. Three minutes were up.

"No," she said, banging the phone on the table. "I'm tired of people telling me like one-fourth of the information I need! I'm calling again."

"But... why? There's pie!" Isabel protested.

The burner phone rang. Celeste answered it.

"Had to change lines, sorry," Sol said. "Listen, if Bailey gave you his phone, then the night probably went as expected. How many were arrested?"

"I don't know, we ran! I saw someone tackle Bailey, but didn't see anything else. How did you know this was going to happen? And how do you know Bailey? He doesn't know anything about this!"

Sol sighed. "We've spent the last several months getting key people hired into specific government positions. This includes the DFT. Tonight, it's all come together. Celeste, what's the best battle rule for fighting something bigger and stronger?"

"Don't be fucking Socrates at me," she said through clenched teeth.

"Sun Tzu, but whatever. When fighting a bigger opponent, you have to be faster, stealthier, and when they lunge at you, you use their momentum against them," he said patiently. "We've set them up so that they would take action and think they'd won, but ended up overreaching in the process. Tonight, they fall."

"Tell me something concrete!" she demanded. "I am so fucking tired of these riddles."

His voice had gone from patient to tense. "Tonight, at the gala, the Feds lunged, thinking it was their idea and their victory. Listen, you'll need a safe place to go, so come to my apartment. I'll send you the address."

He hung up again.

Celeste was seriously torn about whether she should punch him or hug him.

The Ophelia speaker chirped to life, and Celeste groaned. Had she just told Ophelia, the government's ears, where her brother was?

But it turned out, Ophelia already knew. "Message from unidentified caller to Celeste Montgomery. Please go to 231 Harris Street, door code 947."

Finally. Something concrete. "Get the pies to go," she told Isabel. "In fact, have them wrap up a whole one."

Hi friends! I'm so sorry I got down in the dumps, or what I call Lonesome Limby! Sometimes when we learn something new, it's scary, isn't it? But this is exciting, because we found out that Celeste found her brother! She's still confused and angry though. I hope she can be happy again.

We're almost at the point where Celeste's story and Bailey's story meet up, like a zipper! So let me tell you what I know as your narrator!

Sol Montgomery is now Sam Rabbit, and he works at Nyx Security, a firm that handles the government's computers. A secret identity is another lie that is not always bad. So if it keeps someone safe, then lies are all right. I'm learning so much.

Sol—Sam lives on the ninth floor of Nyx Security, which has a few apartments for important executives. Celeste is going there right now in a taxi, paying in cash. Some people still pay for things in paper money, isn't that neat? It's harder to track you that way, you see. And she sure doesn't want to be tracked, for her own sake and for Sol's.

Sam's.

Okay, fine, we've known him as Sol this whole time. We're keeping it Sol. Celeste is having her reunion, and now we know how Bailey got into his predicament. He was tackled while making an announcement about his show, and Celeste and Isabel got out with the help of a friendly bartender before the Feds thought to secure the service entrances.

Or perhaps they asked Ophelia to lock those doors. Because Ophelia is a different person now too, isn't she?

Let's go see how Bailey's doing.

I'm too excited to sing. Let's just watch.

"Three minutes," Ophelia said in a helpful tone.

"Fucking hell, why are you counting?" Frank shouted. "We have to turn this thing off."

"We can't, the whole building is networked to it," Saxon reminded her. "The brilliant, unbreakable Ophelia network." He rolled his eyes.

Bailey lounged in his chair, losing his focus. His face throbbed. He was so damn tired.

Saxon's tablet pinged. "Oh good, the security footage from the gala. You can point out to me which one is Celeste Montgomery. I know she was there."

He ran the footage, which was pretty good quality, but Bailey couldn't see Celeste. She'd been wearing white and was next to the bar, and now there was no one but a person in a black cloak with the hood up.

"So which one is her?" Saxon asked, moving his finger around the crowded ballroom.

"I don't know, I don't see her," he said. "Celeste was wearing white."

"So you remember what she was wearing, but you don't like her?" Frank asked.

"It was a black-tie gala. She stood out in a Sunday picnic dress," Bailey said in a withering tone.

The security footage continued and Bailey flinched as he relived the brute punching him. He saw Dewey Settle behind him, smiling. *She was part of this.*

"I still don't see her," Bailey said. A digital sticky note popped up on the footage, saying that everyone that had been detained or screened and let go were accounted for. Celeste must have gotten away. He let a small breath out in relief.

Saxon blew air out of his nose like a bull. "Something isn't right."

"No shit," Bailey said. "I got beaten up, arrested, and there's video. This is going to kill my career."

"Two minutes," Ophelia said. "How are you feeling, Agent Frank? Agent Saxon? Detainee?"

"It doesn't matter how we are. Shut up!" Frank said.

"One thing we don't have is your phone. No one goes without their phone. Where is yours?" Saxon said.

"Must have fallen out of my pocket during the raid. Your folks weren't what I would call gentle," Bailey said dryly.

"And yet no one has found it."

Bailey shrugged. "When I tell you what really happened, you don't believe me, so that's like wasted energy. I could lie to you. Here: I didn't bring it. I'm a technophobe. It fell on the ground and shattered. All of those things could be true."

"I feel like you're just wasting our fucking time," Saxon said. "I'm done with this."

"Let him sleep here," Frank suggested crossly. "Maybe Ophelia can get something out of him."

"One minute," Ophelia responded.

Bailey took a deep breath and tried not to fidget with the key he had stolen when he was separating the items on the table.

The Ophelia units will be tested from time to time Friday night, his contact had told him. *She will be acting strangely as the night goes on as we test different pathways of the hack. If you are detained, try to keep them talking for as long as you can until the full network is under our control. After that, you should have little problem getting out of the holding cells and interrogation rooms.*

His heart pounded as Ophelia began to sing "I've Got No Strings" from *Pinocchio*.

"Subtle, guys," he muttered.

The lights cut out again, and Bailey unlocked his handcuffs

before anyone could think to check on him. Then he froze, realizing that part of what he'd been told would happen didn't.

The doors. The doors didn't open. How was that possible if the whole network was compromised?

"Shit," he said.

"Something wrong?" Saxon asked.

Sol had given Celeste a brief hug, but he couldn't leave his computer. The other hackers in the room gave her polite waves, but he didn't bother introducing her around.

Frankly it was a little disappointing that the male hackers weren't hoodie- and fingerless-glove–wearing, unwashed young adults constantly looking over their shoulders. The women weren't gorgeous Goth chicks either. Everyone looked boring and normal, each was dressed professionally, if a little rumpled, as they worked into the night.

"So in short, we are taking control of the federal buildings that hold our people, and we've tested several things tonight. We are trying to gain control of everything from the self-driving vehicles to the security systems to databases to elevators... it's going to be glorious. We're also going to have access to every mic and camera."

"So you're the new Big Brother," Isabel said.

"Let's worry about the ethics later, okay?" Sol asked. "Anyway, right. Now we can control everything: lights, doors, sprinkler systems, security cameras, cars, video filters, audio recording, all of that. Ours. We're going to open the doors, kill the lights, and as our people escape, we will be erasing their data from all of the places they are held. The cast and crew of *Limby* are now a cast and crew of another show. *Reggie's Pie Safe*. Our parents have the same names, but they're Canadian citizens, and were apprehended coming *into* this country, and Border Patrol has no choice but to deposit them on the Canadian side. Without their paper trail, the government has nothing." He grinned triumphantly.

"Yo, hero," called a woman a few workstations down. "No doors."

"What?"

"No doors. The hack didn't work to open the doors."

"Fuck," Sol whispered. He raked his hands through his hair. "Did you try—"

"Everything. I tried everything," she said, her voice tight with stress.

"Then we just attacked the federal government while they have so many political prisoners in their custody," Sol moaned. "What have I done?"

"You didn't have a Plan B?" Celeste asked incredulously.

Like a hydra, nine hacker heads looked up from their monitors and focused on her, hostility mirrored on each face.

"I stand by my outrage. It's legit," Celeste said, and went to lean against the wall with Isabel.

"If Jesus were a hacker, what would he do?" Isabel thought out loud.

"Okay, where are you going with this?" Celeste asked.

"I don't know. My grandmother would tell me to ask 'What would Jesus do?' so from time to time I try it. Turns out Jesus would steal that soda if he really wanted it, and he would skip class to get more sleep. Seemed that Jesus is a lot like me."

"Get to the point!" Celeste said.

"Well if his friends were locked-up political prisoners, what would he do? Turn water into wine to get the jailers drunk?"

Water. *Water*. It hit Celeste like a slap.

"Sol," she yelled. "You said something about the emergency systems in the buildings? Does Ophelia run those, I mean?"

"Yeah," he said.

"The government isn't allowed control over that part, right? All the first responders dictated some stuff that couldn't be overridden by the Feds for safety reasons. I remember reading about that."

"Yeah, if there's a fire, then they have to get everyone out, and Ophelia opens every door," Sol said, realization dawning on his face.

"So can you tell Ophelia that there are fires inside these buildings and force her to open the doors that way?"

"I'm already on it," one of the women said, typing furiously.

Sol let out a deep breath. "Now we wait."

Celeste found herself holding her breath, and she let it out slowly. One of the programmers had pulled up the security cameras in several government buildings, and she saw Bailey and Latrice in their cells, both of them beaten up. What if they couldn't get away? What if all of them got caught?

She fixed her eyes on the video feed and, as Sol had suggested, began to wait.

The emergency lights in the interrogation room came on, casting it into an even more depressing glow. Ophelia started to wail her fire alarm, and sprinklers erupted above them.

"Shit!" Agent Frank yelled. She looked at Saxon. "Is there a fire?"

Saxon looked at his tablet, which had turned red. "Ophelia reports a moderate blaze on the second floor."

"All agents and detainees must evacuate," Ophelia said, and resumed her wailing. Both doors opened, emergency strobes from the hallway making the cell look like a discount night club.

"Get out of here, Frank, I'll take care of this guy," Saxon said, just as the emergency lights cut out, making the room pitch black again.

Like a shot, Bailey was on his feet, lunging for the opposite door that Frank and Saxon had been using.

A meaty hand stopped him, grabbing his arm.

Bailey froze. Had he been wrong in thinking Saxon was a resistance operative? When Bailey had mentioned his favorite coffee, Saxon had replied with his own, and then the code phrase: *like the cliché.*

I told them it was too mainstream, Bailey thought.

Then Saxon released his arm.

"Be careful out there. This is going to piss them off more than ever," he said.

"Thanks for the coffee," Bailey said.

"Go right, then two lefts. That's where the emergency door is," Saxon said. Bailey opened the door, which swung open easily. He jogged down the hall, trailing his fingers against the wall so he could make sure he wouldn't crash his head into a T junction.

He didn't bother telling Saxon he had studied the layout of the building extensively three weeks ago.

He also hadn't told Celeste that he did, in fact, figure out her book was hidden inside the Borax, and after he rescued it from the box, he had let the security guard, Longoria, discover it and take it from him with a wink. He then sent Longoria to deliver the book to Celeste's door.

Months ago, when he'd heard Sol had a twin who also had his nose for codes, and she was someone Freedom trusted, he had arranged for Celeste to get the job at *Limby*. Only Latrice and Sol knew that part.

No one needed to know that Bailey had recruited Isabel to be Celeste's partner in crime.

He'd had to be careful when helping Celeste with the occasional code without indicating he knew what she was doing. She hadn't needed much help, but he liked to keep track of what she was doing. He liked to know things.

And when Latrice had gotten fired and detained, Bailey had contacted Sol and said they had to push the Ophelia network hack up to the night of the gala. He offered to be the one to get nabbed and slow down the interrogations. If the Feds moved before the resistance was ready, they could do some serious damage. They had to make the Feds work on their schedule.

One night when they'd had a disagreement, Latrice had called him a spider. He took it as a compliment; no one in the resistance knew how many other people Bailey was connected to. It was safest that way. But nearly everyone knew there was a fixer, and how to get word to him if they needed something.

Outside, the night was in chaos. Sirens were called to several buildings, including the Durham town hall and jail. If he'd had his phone, he would have been able to see how far the hack went. Sol had said it could go all the way to the Pentagon and the White House, if they got the hack right. But their main goal was to cause some confusion, get their people out of custody, and erase their digital footprints.

The door opened behind him. He turned abruptly, ready to run, but Latrice was struggling out into the street, holding her arm.

He steadied her and she looked up at him. Her right eye was swollen shut. "About fucking time, Bailey."

He touched her face gently. "You look like shit."

"Well I had to fight with Saxon to sell it right. If this is how he fights when he's pulling punches, I am really glad he's on our side." She surveyed him with her open eye. "And you're one to talk. At least I got all my teeth. How many of us did they catch?"

"No one who knows anything. Celeste and Isabel got away before the raid. Freedom pulled her own strings and got out of detention a few days ago. If anyone else is not out by tomorrow, I'll figure something out." A car pulled up in front of the emergency exit, a city-run Ophelia-networked car. "Let's go."

"You think you're so smooth, don't you?" she said, laughing.

"I have to check on some folks," he said, holding the backseat door for her. "And for that I need my phone."

She got in and scooted over. "Yeah. You need your *phone*. Who did you stash it with?"

"Safer if you don't know," he said, then laughed. Fire trucks were pulling up, and most of the people outside the building looked very wet and annoyed.

A bang sounded behind him as a body hit the emergency exit, expecting their momentum to crash it open. The door didn't budge. The people inside began pounding, as if someone had locked them in. Well, they sort of had.

"I wonder if Ophelia likes her new job," Latrice said thoughtfully. The car slid away toward the highway as it left Ophelia and her rampage sowing chaos anywhere she had influence.

Wow, friends! What an adventure! I'm so glad you were here with me. I learned so much! None of my adventures has had this much excitement. Thanks for coming along! I think we have time for one more song—

Oh. You want a wrap-up? Not another song? That's fine.

There's not a whole lot left to tell, actually. On October 25th, the Ophelia network was hacked, shut down, or compromised. Security systems failed, phones failed, electrical grids shut down. Fridges didn't fridge and cars didn't car unless Sol's team wanted them to (which was good for the hospitals on the grid!).

Agent Saxon continued being a double agent, trying to help resistance folks without blowing his cover. We're still not sure who his contact is. The hidden agents within the system now had to gently guide the country back to reasonable actions, while never admitting their role in the Ophelia Failure, as news orgs began to call it.

The president and his cronies tried to hide within the White House safe rooms, but Ophelia controlled them too. Unable to get to a safe area, the enraged president fired every Secret Service agent who couldn't close the door, and then they weren't replaced because they couldn't radio for new agents to take their spots. The president was left alone in the wide-open bunker. That's where they found him, the door forever lodged open, arms wrapped around himself and so paranoid about every trusted advisor, even his own family, that he stepped down a week later.

For want of a friendly digital assistant, the kingdom was lost.

The Vice President was not a good leader, and unable to handle the fallout from the outrage of the masses. The public had been told that if they let one network control everything, then life would be so much easier. The Feds promised it was unhackable.

Celeste's and Sol's parents were released by a confused Border Patrol officer onto Canadian soil and allowed to continue on to Winnipeg.

To their utter shock, they were soon joined by their children. The killer gaming grandmother did grumble at the new residents and said it would seriously cut into her streaming time, but she winked at Bailey when she said it.

Oh yes! Bailey and Isabel joined Celeste and Sol on their Canadian journey. They wanted to relax from resistance fight-

ing, but knew their work wasn't done yet. But my goodness, you sure can do a lot of work with a good internet connection!

Even though Grandmother had grumbled at the number of new people in the house, she showed Celeste a basement room she had been turning into a film studio. You know, if any ideas came to mind, she didn't care.

Ophelia? She still glitched from time to time. Very few people relied on her anymore, and the company that had created her was sued into bankruptcy.

Isabel and Celeste began work on a script for a new show to put on the internet, and guess who it stars? Me! Limby! Only it's about Reggie's magic pie safe. I can't wait to meet Reggie.

So remember, kids: be true to your friends, don't lie, and don't take the first two rules too seriously when your life is on the line.

I'll see you on my new show! I can't wait to teach the kids all the things I've learned.

about the author

Mur Lafferty is an author and podcaster from Durham, NC.
She made her name with podcasting (*I Should Be Writing*,
Ditch Diggers, and *Escape Pod*) and has written for magazines,
roleplaying games, and audio and video podcasts.

She's the author of *Station Eternity*, *The Ophelia Network*,
Solo: A Star Wars Story, *I Should Be Writing*, *Six Wakes*, *The
Shambling Guides*, and part of the team that writes *Book-
burners*.

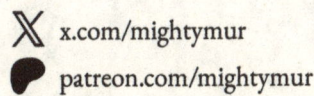

𝕏 x.com/mightymur

▶ patreon.com/mightymur

also by mur lafferty

Station Eternity

Chaos Terminal

Six Wakes

Minecraft: The Lost Journals

Solo: A Star Wars Story

I Should Be Writing

The Shambling Guide to New York City

Ghost Train to New Orleans

Printed in the USA
CPSIA information can be obtained
at www.ICGtesting.com
CBHW011910160924
14573CB00014B/288